P9-CCS-829

/
M2232m

MAC

John MacLean

Houghton Mifflin Company
Boston   1987

To Polly
with love

Library of Congress Cataloging-in-Publication Data

MacLean, John, 1945–
  Mac.

  Summary: Fifteen-year-old Mac's personality
undergoes a sudden change as he tries to come
to terms with the trauma of being sexually abused by
a doctor during a physical examination.
  [1. Child molesting—Fiction.   2. Emotional
problems—Fiction.   3. High schools—Fiction.
4. Schools—Fiction]   I. Title.
PZ7.M22434Mac   1987   [Fic]   87-16994
ISBN 0-395-43080-1

Printed in the United States of America

P   10 9 8 7 6 5 4 3 2 1

The author is grateful for permission to quote from "So Far Away" and
"Why Worry," by Mark Knopfler. Copyright © 1985 by
Chariscourt Limited (PRS). Used by permission of Almo Music Corp.,
Hollywood, California. All rights reserved.

*This is a work of fiction, and all of the characters
in this book are fictional.*

· ONE ·

It's between math and study. Three of us are walking down the hall when she comes out of biology and walks right by us.

"Hi." She smiles at us.

"Hi." We all answer together. She's so pretty I have to look down at the floor. Just looking at her face makes my eyes water. Like looking into the sun or something. But out of the top of my eyes I see she's got shiny black hair. High cheekbones. Eyes kind of unusual, Oriental.

We keep walking without one of us daring to look back. Until we get to the door of the library. When we turn around she's gone.

"You see that?" Woody jams his thumb into his chest. "She said hi to me."

"You?" Shawn laughs. "She was saying hi to me."

"That's a joke," Woody snorts.

"I thought she was saying hi to all of us," I suggest.

"Don't be dumb, Mac." Woody stares down at me. "Don't you know anything about women? They don't go around saying hi to everybody. They say hi to one person at a time. And she was saying hi to me. Didn't you see her eyes?"

"I don't know anything about women." I shrug my shoulders. "All I know is that she's a girl."

"A girl?" Woody is exasperated with me. He has to rest one of his big hands on my shoulder to show me how dumb I am. "Don't you know anything about the facts

3

of life, Mac? Girls play with dolls. Now women, like Jenny —"

"That's her name?" I interrupt. "How do you know her name?"

"What do you mean, how do I know her name? Everyone knows her name."

"Yeah?"

"Yeah. Besides, don't interrupt me when I'm talking."

"Excuse me."

"Just this once. So what was I saying?"

"Girls play with dolls," Shawn reminds him.

"Right. But women like Jenny play with me."

"Hah." Shawn laughs stupidly.

"Not funny, Woody." I knock his hand off my shoulder. "She's only fourteen."

"And you and I are fourteen." He keeps talking.

But I don't listen. I walk into the library. Where it's so quiet I can hear static electricity. I pick up a magazine. Sit down at one of the tables. And begin to thumb through it. But the words and pictures all blur. And all I can do is listen to myself breathe and think about her and guys like Woody. Why do I get so pissed at him? When he's supposed to be my friend. It's just that some of the things he says get to me.

"What are you reading?" It's Woody whispering in my ear. He sits down next to me.

"I don't know." I flip over the magazine. It's *Paris Match*. On the cover is a picture of a beach. And all these women lying around in bikinis.

"Let me see that." He grabs the magazine from me.

And starts thumbing through it. "How about that? Côte d'Azur."

"Where's that?"

"France, man. On the Mediterranean. Don't you know anything? What do I gotta do? Draw pictures for you? Will you look at these chicks, Mac? Just lying there for the taking."

I don't answer him. But stare up at the clock on the wall and figure I have twenty minutes until my next class.

"I figure we'll go to the movies Friday." He leans against my shoulder and whispers into my ear.

"Who's we?" I ask. Like I don't know.

"Me and Jenny."

"Good for you."

"Will you take a look at this?" He pushes the magazine in front of my face. There's a picture of a woman in a bathing suit. Cut so high it makes her legs look like they start under her arms.

"I'd like to see Jenny in that." He taps the page with the back of his hand.

I push the magazine back at him. And don't say anything.

"Ah, I can't take it." He breathes heavily into my ear. "I can't wait until Friday night."

"Why?" I ask. Furious at myself for being so dumb.

"To make out. You jerk. To make out."

• 2 •

Next period is civics. Downstairs in the small room across from the janitor's office. Outside the office window, covered with a dirty green Venetian blind, is an old red and white Coke machine. That hums and rattles and sweats all day long.

I sit in the back trying hard not to confuse the Coke machine with Mrs. Miller's voice. It's not that she's boring, or that I'm not interested in the difference between cameral and bicameral chambers. It's just that I've got other things on my mind. On the wall next to me I notice the world map with all its pinks and blues. And try to find the Côte d'Azur and Saint-Tropez. First I find the Mediterranean. It's sky blue. But then instead of the map I see the pictures in *Paris Match*. French girls in bikinis. And then I'm gone. Daydreaming. I can almost hear the sound of the water lapping against the beach. And then right in front of me is Jenny in hardly a blue bikini. It's like having the wind knocked out of me. I can even smell her suntan lotion. And see little drops of perspiration over her lips and cheeks. Her hair is pulled back in a ponytail. And she's saying something to me. I've got to strain to hear her.

"Do you want to swim?" she whispers.

"Oh, no, I can't," I whisper back. "I've got my school clothes on."

"Take them off."

"I can't do that." I shake my head all embarrassed. "Besides, I'm in class."

"Who cares?"

"Who cares?" I ask out loud.

"What was that, Mac?" Mrs. Miller interrupts from the front of the room. "I didn't hear your question."

I look up from the floor and stare at Mrs. Miller. She's a

nice lady with gray hair and a double chin that shakes when she talks. But when I catch her eye a cold shiver like a piece of ice runs down my spine. "I'm sorry," I say, watching her face bobbing between the kids' heads as she moves towards me.

"You had a question?"

"Ah. You answered it," I lie.

"Well, that's nice." She turns back to the rest of the class. "Now, class, as I was saying, a bicameral chamber . . ."

I take a big breath and look out of the corner of my eye to see if she's still there. But she's gone. The beach is empty except for a few white pebbles and some older women sitting on folding beach chairs. Where'd she go? I look all around the room but there's nothing but kids hiding behind civics books. I close my eyes to try and get her back. But there's nothing. It's times like this that school is depressing.

I look down at my civics notes. The page is empty. I rip it out of the notebook and fold it lengthwise. What I need, I am thinking, is an airplane. Something like the Concorde jet to whip over to Saint-Tropez. Or wherever she went. I fold the paper until it is as streamlined as a missile. I tap the nose of the rocket lightly on the desktop to check for balance. Thinking how surprised and impressed she'll be when I land this thing on the beach. When I look up from my desk to check the flight conditions, kids are looking at me with stupid grins on their faces. That's when I know I'm in trouble.

Somewhere off in the distance Mrs. Miller is circling towards me. In my bones I can feel her moving closer to me. I drop the plane and reach down to tie my running shoes. The Coke machine is gurgling louder than ever. When I sit up from my laces she's standing there right next to my desk. Wearing a faded gray-green dress. With funny little belt loops. A matching belt. And a buckle that's broken.

"So, Mac, you've made an airplane?"

"Well, ah, not exactly." The buckle is missing its center piece.

"Oh. Then perhaps it's a missile? And you thought we were moving from state government to the arms race?"

"I, ah, sort of . . ." I don't know how her belt can stay so snug with a broken buckle. "I was thinking of international . . ." Unless it's the small green thumbtack pushed through the overlapping belt ends.

"International what?" Her voice is stern.

"The, ah, international question." I look up from the belt buckle to her face. It's a kind face. It gives no hint of the pain of thumbtacks.

"About?" Her voice is patient.

"I was wondering." About the thumbtack through the belt.

"Yes?"

"I forget." The class explodes with laughter. I turn red.

"Perhaps you were wondering if this missile of yours can fly? What do you think?"

"I don't think so."

"Let us see."

She takes the airplane off my desk and walks over to the

8

wastebasket. She drops it and it disappears without a sound.

"You're right, Mac." The class laughs louder. I feel my face turning even redder. "Now, suppose from now on, Mac, you work on things that have a chance of flying. Like, for instance, bicameral chambers."

"Yes, Ma'am."

"And let's leave paper airplanes to the airheads."

"Yes, Ma'am."

"Now, class, that's quite enough laughing. Where were we? Who knows? The state house or JFK International Airport?"

• 3 •

Lunch has got to be my favorite period. I cruise upstairs to my locker. Trying not to think about civics and Mrs. Miller. Or the lecture she gave me after class. "You have to keep your mind from wandering, Mac!" I just nodded my head. "That's not like you." I nodded my head some more. "Do you want to tell me what you were thinking about?" No thanks!

I jump up the last set of stairs, two at a time. And cruise down the corridor. It's lined with lockers. Mine is at the other end. And I am starving to death. When I finally get to it I spin the combination lock. Yank open the door. And grab my lunch. We're not allowed to eat at our lockers. School rules. But there's so much noise and so many kids. Who's gonna notice? I reach in the brown bag and break off a piece of egg salad sandwich. Pop it in my mouth. And crumple the bag closed.

"Hi." I hear a girl's voice a few lockers away. I stop chewing. Kick the locker door closed. And turn to see who it is.

It's her! And she's looking at me. I look down at the floor. Then stare at my closed locker. My mind scrambles. Like eggs. Like I've lost my breath or something. Out of the corner of my eye I look down the row of lockers to see who she could be talking to. Nobody's there! I look across the corridor. No one's there either. I try and swallow the sandwich. Without choking. I can feel my ears turning red. She's talking to me.

"Hi," I mumble through the egg salad. What else can I say? But I can't think of a thing. So I mumble hi again. And try to look up from her blue running shoes.

"Hi." She closes her locker door, turns, and smiles. I feel like I'm going to melt. Right in front of her. And that will be the end of me. Just a puddle at the foot of my locker. I swallow the egg salad. I've got to say something. Any second she's gonna be gone. And I'll never see her again.

"Want a bite?" I hold out an apple from my bag.

"No, thanks." She shakes her head. "I have to go."

I take a big bite out of the apple to show her how relaxed I am.

"Yeah," I mumble around the apple. "Me too."

She starts to walk away.

"So, how do you like your locker?" I ask, taking another bite out of the apple as she walks by.

"What did you say?" She stops. And tilts her head to one side so that her black hair falls across her shoulder. Like she can't believe my question. I can't believe it either. "What did you say?"

"I, ah ... being new and all ... you are new aren't you?" I stumble over words like I never used them before. "I was wondering if you like the lockers here, ah, better than at your old school."

"A locker's a locker." And she starts back down the corridor.

"Yeah." I take another bite of the apple. "A locker's a locker." I'm not too stupid. I stand there eating around the core of the apple. Watching her disappear down the hall. Then I start for the cafeteria. Slowly at first. Then suddenly sprinting down the hallway between the other kids until I can feel blood rising to my face. And I can pretend it has something to do with the running.

• 4 •

"I think Jenny loves me." Woody smiles across the white plastic tabletop at me, Brook, and Shawn. It's been a couple of weeks since we first saw her. I don't say a word. Even though I'd like to strangle him.

"Why is it that sometimes you're such a pain in the ass, Woody?" Shawn takes a bite out of his peanut butter sandwich. A glob of red jam oozes out the side of his mouth.

"You're jealous, Shawn. You're just jealous 'cause I'm

state of the art." I watch him rip open a can of Mountain Dew. Lean back. And pour it down his throat. I guess he is state of the art. I mean he shaves. He's over six feet. And has an Adam's apple. I watch it bobbing up and down as he drinks. And he isn't afraid to talk to girls. They probably even think he's cute.

"Jealous?" Shawn drops his sandwich down on the table. Like it's disgusting or something. "Of you? You've got to be kidding." He wipes the jam off his face with the back of his hand.

"So how do you know she loves you?" Brook asks.

"Yeah?" I echo. Brook is sitting next to me picking at a thing of cottage cheese with a white plastic fork. His parents are slowly starving him to death. All they ever give him for lunch is junk like plain yogurt, sprouts, tofu, and soybeans ground up like hamburger. Nothing but crap. That's why he's skinnier than a straw. And why he's always picking off of our plates.

"What'd you say?" Woody finishes his Mountain Dew and looks across the table at Brook and me.

"I said, how do you know she loves you?" Brook pushes his cottage cheese towards me. And reaches in my Thermos for a piece of ravioli.

"How do I know she loves me?" Woody repeats. Rips open the cellophane wrapper of an eighty-cent chocolate chip cookie. And takes a bite. We watch him chew. Waiting. The cafeteria is not a quiet place. Kids are always standing up and sitting down. Chairs getting scraped in and out. Trays getting dropped. And everyone talking at once. Except at our table. We're just waiting and listening. I look around the room. Without looking like I'm looking. Wondering where she is.

"I said, how come she loves you?" Brook repeats his question as he finishes off my ravioli.

"I know what you said." Woody wipes his mouth. "And the answer is, pencil face, because she's going out with me."

"Bullshit." Shawn crumples his crust in his fist. "That's bullshit."

"See. I told you. You're jealous."

"That'll be the day." Shawn throws the wadded crust at Woody.

"So where you taking her?" Brook asks.

"What does that matter?" Woody rips open a bag of peanuts and hands a single peanut to Brook. "Here you go, skin and bones."

"So where you going?" I repeat Brook's question.

"None of your business."

"So when did you ask her?" Brook pulls the cottage cheese back in front of him and picks at one of the curds.

"You guys are really something." Woody shakes his head. "What do you want from me? A docudrama? Or what?"

"Try the truth," Shawn mutters.

"The truth is," Woody smiles at us, "she's going out with me. So that must mean she loves me. I mean, I'm just one state-of-the-art kind of guy. I mean, am I right or am I wrong?"

I lie in bed that night thinking. I've got on my headphones and am listening to some Genesis. Thinking. I'm not a state-of-the-art guy. I mean, I like my family. Even though sometimes I try not to. My mom's a lawyer. My dad's a househusband. Not really too state of the art. And me. I'm maybe five nine. A hundred and forty pounds. Kind of blond, curly hair. Nothing like Woody. Or some of the older kids. Just kind of boring. I mean, I wake up in the morning. Go to school. Play soccer. Come home. Eat supper. Do homework. Go to bed. And that's it. Nothing special.

And not too swift. Especially with girls. I proved that today. "Hi. Want a bite of my apple? How do you like your locker?" Such stupidity sends shivers up and down my spine. I mean, how can one jerk be so stupid? Her locker's only two or three away from mine. What am I going to do the rest of the year? I'm going to run out of apples. I've got to think of something to say. But what? What would a state-of-the-art guy say? How should I know? My mind's as empty as a blank tape. There's nothing there except for Genesis.

I turn off the tape. Hang the headphones on the end of my bed. And roll over and try and go to sleep. But I can't. I keep thinking about Jenny. Not daydreaming or stuff like that. It's just like she's around. Kind of like a shadow. Even when I think I'm thinking about other things. She's right there.

I roll over and stare at the ceiling. Then at the fish tank at the end of my bed. The light's off. But the heater makes a red glow. I watch the angelfish, staring off into space. Wondering what I'm ever gonna think of to say to her. I don't know how long I watch the fish. The next thing I know it's morning. And the alarm is buzzing a hole through my head.

· 6 ·

We're sitting around a cafeteria table. Not saying much. It's Friday. Not such a bad day. Except it's the end of the week and we kind of run out of things to say. Same table. Same guys. Eating the same junk. We're just sitting there. Spacing out. Listening to the noise of five hundred kids. When Brook jumps up and yells, "Hey, Pogo. It's Pogo."

"Big deal." Woody jabs a straw into a piece of bread. "Don't wet your pants, Brook."

Pogo's a twelfth-grader. But he talks to us. Always setting us straight on what to do. What to say. He's kind of granola different, though. I mean, he has long hair and talks old-fashioned.

"Hey, little dudes, what's new?" He puts an empty tray on our table. Spins a chair around and sits in it backwards.

"Hey, Pogo." We all smile.

"Where's your lunch?" Shawn asks.

"Smoked it." He rubs a hand over his chin. So we can hear how rough his beard is. We all laugh, sort of nervously.

"You high?" Woody asks without moving his lips.

"What'd you say?" Pogo puts a hand to his ear.

Woody smiles at me. Looks around the room real quick like he's looking for teachers.

"You high?" he whispers a little louder.

"Totally."

"What'd you smoke?" Woody bounces his eyebrows up and down. Like it's a big conspiracy.

"Tuna on rye." Pogo slaps the table with his hand so that our trays jump. We laugh. Not because it's funny, but because that's what we're supposed to do. Twelfth-graders are always a riot. Even Woody laughs. Then he puts the straw in his mouth and blows a piece of bread across the table at Shawn. But it doesn't get halfway.

"So what's happening with you little dudes? You guys got a soccer game today? Or what?"

"Yeah," I answer. "Against Swift River."

"All right. Take it to them. Maybe I'll catch this one."

"Thanks." Shawn picks up a milk carton and holds it up over his mouth. He gets a couple of drops.

"So what's happening this weekend? Any action?" Pogo asks. Nobody answers.

"What about you, Mac? What you doing?"

"Nothing."

"You guys." He shakes his head. Like he's really disappointed.

"Woody's got a date." Shawn's still holding the milk carton over his mouth.

"Shut up, Shawn." Woody jabs the straw in the piece of

bread and blows another bread bomb at him. This time it nearly makes it across the table.

"Is that right? Well, all right. So who's the lucky lady?"

"New girl," Shawn answers. He's smiling and looking at Woody out of the corner of his eye.

"I said shut up, Shawn."

"Who?" Pogo puts a hand to his ear.

"Make me." Shawn puts the carton down and stares straight at Woody. "He says he's going out with Jenny."

"The new girl." Pogo nods his head. "Interesting." He says it real slow. Like he knows something we don't.

"What do you mean?" Woody hits the straw against his hand like it's a cigarette.

"I only mean that you're the fifth guy who tells me he's taking her out tonight."

"Screw you, Pogo." Woody throws the straw across the table at Shawn. Like it's all his fault.

"Hey." Pogo holds both his hands up in the air like he's parking cars or something. "I'm just telling you."

"So who are all these jerks?" Woody is getting red around the lips and ears.

"Hey, who am I to say? Just a bunch of seniors. What do I know?"

"Figures." Woody picks up his tray like he's leaving.

"Why don't they pick on girls their own age?" I say. I look at Pogo, then at Woody. Embarrassed I said anything.

"Hey." Pogo holds his hands up again. "She's fourteen. It's a free world."

"Yeah?" I want to shut up, but I don't. It's like my mouth talks without me. "I call it robbing the cradle."

"Hey, little dude, your time will come," Pogo scolds me. Then he turns to Woody. "So listen. I mean, if you and Jenny are going out tonight? I'm throwing a party. The parents are away. So swing by and we'll show you how the big guys play."

"Yeah?" Woody stands up and pushes his chair under the table. "Maybe I will."

"Excellent." Pogo and Shawn pick up their trays. And the three of them leave Brook and me sitting alone at the table.

"Guess she's in demand," Brook says, as he reaches over and starts unscrewing my Thermos.

"Cool it." I slap his hand away.

"Jeez. You're touchy today."

"Yeah? Well, I just get tired of feeding you sometimes. Okay?"

"Well, excuse me." He gets up and leaves. I don't. I just sit there. Listening to the sounds of everyone else leaving.

• 7 •

I usually go from last period right to the gym. Except on game days. Then I always go to my locker to make sure I haven't forgotten anything. Like my goalie gloves or elbow pads.

I walk down the hall. It's empty and quiet. A few kids are at their lockers. The rest have gone home or are at the gym. I turn a corner and start for my locker, thinking only about the game, when I spot her. She's standing right in front of her locker. Her head is bent to one side so that her straight black hair falls over her shoulder like a scarf. I stop walking. My heart starts pounding. Like it's already the beginning of the game or something. I turn and start back the way I came. Thinking I got everything. But I only take a few steps. Stop again. What am I doing? I always check my locker before a game. What if I don't this time? Against our biggest rival? I turn around and start back towards her. If I walk quickly maybe she won't notice me. I walk on my tiptoes up to my locker. I don't dare look at her. I slide my book bag onto the floor. And like a safe-cracker, turn the combination lock. It ticks quietly in my hands before it unlocks. Then the door squeaks open. I stare into the locker. Empty, except for a pile of old papers and my elbow pads. I pull them up over my elbows. Shut the door. And start to leave.

"Excuse me. Can you help me a minute?"

"I, ah, have to go to a game," I say to the wall.

"My locker won't open," she says.

I turn and look down at the floor.

"Something's wrong with the lock," she says. Then pointing to the elbow pads asks, "What's wrong with your arm?" I look at her hand. Then at the pad. Like there can't possibly be a connection. Then out of nowhere an answer floats into my mind.

"Nothing. It's for soccer. We have a game today."

"Oh. Well, do you think you could help me with this

lock?" She backs away from her locker to make room for me. I shrug my shoulders. Step in front of her locker and she whispers the combination to me. Her voice sends chills up and down my spine. I spin the dial dizzily. Yank it open. But it doesn't budge. I try two more times.

"It won't open." I feel like an idiot. "You sure this is the right one?" I turn and look at her real quickly. Her eyes slightly slanted. Her lips bare. So that I have to look away.

"Of course I'm sure." She bites at the nail of her right thumb. "Damn. I was going to get all my work done. Now what am I going to do?"

I stare down at the floor at the book bag in front of my locker. I can't believe I'm blowing such an opportunity. And then suddenly, out of nowhere, an idea.

"You could use my books," I mumble to the front of her locker.

"What?" I can feel her looking at me.

"I said, you can use my books while I'm at the game."

"Are they the right ones?"

"You in ninth grade?" I look up at her. She nods. "So use 'em." I pick up the bag and hand it to her.

"You sure?" She takes the bag from me. "But where will I meet you?"

"Meet me?" I can barely say the words.

"To give you your books back."

"Oh. I don't know. The library? After the game?"

"Okay," she says. And for a second our eyes come together. And it's just like a shock. Like when my finger slips and touches the bare metal of an electric plug.

The soccer field is out behind the school. Down by the river. I jog slowly out to the goal. The hills on the other side of the river are intense. Orange, red, and yellow against the blue sky. The grass is dark green. I jump up and touch the white crossbar a couple of times. So that I'll remember where it is. The grass is still wet. It must have rained last night. Not enough to make it muddy. But enough to make the ground soft when I fall. Something I do a lot as goalie.

I can't concentrate the first half. My mind on my books. I have to make a few stops. But mostly the ball dribbles through somebody's legs. All I have to do is fall on it. A real dull first half. No one scores. During halftime the coach gives our forwards and halfbacks hell. Tells them they're sleepwalking. But it isn't until the fourth quarter that they start pressuring the other goal.

It starts with a long pass down the right side. Shawn takes it on his chest. Drops it to his feet. Fakes the fullback inside. Goes outside. And kicks a high looping ball. A goalie's nightmare. It drops over his head into the net. And there's nothing he can do about it. After the goal everyone swarms around Shawn. And there's a lot of high-fiving.

For the rest of the game the ball stays mostly at midfield. Except when a Swift River kid breaks through our fullbacks. And suddenly there he is. Right on top of me.

Too late to cut him off. I have to wait. I crouch down. Try to find his eyes. The coach always says you have to find their eyes. They'll tell you where he's going. Right corner? Left corner? Straight ahead? Suddenly I know he's going left corner. But I don't move. Wait for the foot, the coach says, wait for the foot.

"Shoot, you bastard," I swear under my breath. "Shoot the damn ball." His foot goes back. I start for the left corner. The ball explodes off his foot. Too late, I think. I'm too late. The ball spins towards the corner. I reach out with my left hand. It's curving away from me. I'll never get it. Never!

Something slaps against my glove. I fall to the ground. Did it go in? I don't know where it is! I roll over and try to get to my feet. Then I see it rolling away from me. In front of the open goal. I start scrambling for it. But before I get halfway there I see a foot kicking the ball. I stop. To try and block it. But the ball, instead of exploding past me, dribbles slowly towards my hands. I fall on it. When I look up Brook is standing there. A big smile on his face.

"Thanks, buddy." I smile. "I thought I was dead."

"Nice stop."

"Showboat," Woody screams. He runs up and stands over me to keep Swift River forwards away from the ball. "How come you gotta make the most routine plays look spectacular?"

I don't say anything. I don't even smile. I just get up, dribble the ball a couple of times, and kick it down the right side of the field.

"You see who came to watch me play?" Woody stands

in the middle of the goalie's crease. Like the game's over.

"Hey, get down there." I push him downfield.

"Just look over there." He motions towards the bench with his chin. I look. It's too far to see her face. But I can see her black hair falling over the shoulders of her blue jacket. Suddenly I'm freezing cold.

"See that?" Woody jabs his thumb against his chest. "Tell me I'm not a stud." Then like a sprinter he's never been, he races downfield. Leaving me in the goal shivering. Jumping up and down to stay warm.

• 9 •

When the gun goes off we all run into the middle of the field. High-fiving. Jumping up and down. Yelling and cheering. Slapping each other on the butt. Then we line up single file and shake hands with Swift River. Saying, Good game. Good game.

After the coach gives us his post-game rap he drives off in his red Toyota pickup. I sit on the bench at the edge of the field with Shawn and Brook, and pull on my sweat pants. We're all talking about the game. Except for Woody. He's over by Jenny and some other girls. Waving his arms in the air. Like he's telling jokes or something. I pull on my sweat shirt and loop the hood over my head. Not as cold now. Everyone talks at once. Until Woody starts telling a joke so loud that all the guys on the bench turn around to listen to him.

". . . so these parents had two kids. I don't know, maybe fifteen and seventeen. And the mother's really getting

23

upset about them swearing. Always complaining to the father. So one night he tells her, Tomorrow we're going to put an end to it. I promise. So the next morning they're having a quiet breakfast. The seventeen year old sits down at the table and says, Where the hell are the corn flakes? The father doesn't say anything. But stands up. Walks over to the kid. Grabs him out of his seat. Smacks him in the mouth. Knees him in the gut. And when the kid falls to the floor, he kicks him in the ribs. Then he turns to the fifteen-year-old kid who just walked into the room. Now what do you want? he growls at the kid. The kid looks at his father and then at his brother moaning on the floor and says, You can bet your ass it ain't the corn flakes."

It's a long time before we stop laughing. And by then everyone has a joke they want to tell. Pretty soon the clouds are getting dark and the wind is whipping across the field.

"Let's go the gym," Woody suggests. "It's cold." But I just sit there and watch Jenny and him and the other girls cross the field. Walking up past the baseball diamond. Towards the light over the door of the gym.

"There he goes," I mutter to Brook. "The state-of-the-art guy."

"State-of-the-art ass." Brook stands up. "It's dark. Let's go shower." We get up off the bench and start slowly after them. Walking over the black grass. Towards the light. By the time we get to the gym everyone's gone or inside. I pull open the door. Brook steps into the hall. I start after him.

"Mac?" a voice calls from outside. I turn. And standing

at the edge of the light is Jenny. "Here's your book bag."

"Go get your bag, man." Brook elbows me in the ribs. "You sly guy, you."

"Shut up, Brook," I mutter, with my mouth closed, and swing the door shut on him. I start slowly across the sidewalk towards her. My eyes on the ground.

"Here." She hands me the bag. "Thank you. I got everything done but English."

"You're welcome." I take the bag from her. "You, ah, are . . . can borrow my English book if you want."

"But what about your English?"

"Ah, I already did it." I lie without meaning to.

"Oh." She takes half a step back. I turn and look at the door. It's half open and Brook and a bunch of other guys are peeking through it.

"You guys." I start for the door. I can hear them running down the hall to the locker room. Laughing their stupid heads off.

"It's okay," she calls after me, "if I borrow it?"

"What?" I stop and turn around and then, remembering, grab the English book out of the bag. She steps towards me.

"You sure?"

"Yup." I nod my head. And just stand there. Like an idiot. With nothing to say. She just stands there too. Holding the book.

"It was a fun game." She finally breaks the silence.

"Yeah."

"Fun to watch, I mean." When I look up at her she's

staring out across the parking lot like she's looking for her ride. Then real quietly she says, "You sure played good."

"Thanks." I can barely say the word. I look out towards the parking lot too. Embarrassed.

"I mean, you all played great."

"Yeah." Even more embarrassed, I kick a rock across the sidewalk. She doesn't say anything. We just stand there some more. Looking out into the parking lot. Finally I think of something to ask. "You waiting for your ride?"

"My older brother." She looks at me. "You have any brothers?"

"If you can call them that."

"What do you mean?"

"I have kid brothers."

"So they're your brothers, aren't they?"

"Yeah. I guess. Only sometimes I wish they weren't."

"And I thought you were a nice guy. Lending me your books and everything." She looks at me real sternly. I look down at the sidewalk. Wondering what it was that I said wrong.

"How old are they?" she asks. Taking me by surprise.

"They're both six."

"Both? Are they twins?"

"Yeah."

"That's neat."

"Neat? They're not so neat. They're barbarians. You should try eating with them."

"What do you mean?" She laughs a little. So I go on.

"You know what they think a chair is for?" She shakes her head. "Something to stand next to. Maybe once in a while to put a knee on." She laughs again. So I keep talking. "And usually when they do decide to sit down they miss the chair completely and end up on the floor. When we go out to eat to McDonald's or for pizza? That's the worst. They're either sliding under the tables or standing at the juke box snapping their fingers. So I usually go to another table. Pretend that I don't know them. So what do they do? They wave at me from the juke box. Hiya, Mac, they call, and then they come over and slide under my table." She's laughing all the time now. Like she thinks they're a riot. I can't believe it. I've never made a girl laugh before. And I'm not even trying. I'm just talking about my stupid brothers. It's like she really likes hearing about them. So I keep talking.

"You think it's funny. But what if they were your brothers?"

"They sound so cute."

I look at her in the half-light. She smiles so easily. I smile too. "Cute? You think it's cute? They start off on the chair and then their spines turn to jelly. And the next thing you know they're half on the floor. Half on the chair. Their eyes level to the table. Their heads half-covered with their shirts. And they're looking at each other's belly buttons. And asking me, in their loud little voices, Hey, Mac, you got an inny or an outy?"

"That's so cute." She laughs hard and she isn't faking. I can tell.

"Cute she calls them?" I slap my forehead and spin in a circle.

"Adorable," she laughs.

"Adorable? Listen. You know what they do to my room?" I ask, as a pair of headlights swings into the parking lot.

"No. Tell me," she says, with her soft laugh. I don't answer, but watch the lights swing up towards the sidewalk to the gym.

"Is that your ride?"

"Oh, my ride. Damn. I have to go." She looks at me and makes a funny pout with her lips. "I wanted to hear the end of it."

"There is no end but I'll tell you this story real quick . . . Onceuponatimemylittlebrothers."

"Very funny." She looks at the V.W. bus. Then at me. "Can you call me?"

"Me?"

"Yes, you."

"Why me?" I can't believe I ask such stupid questions.

"To finish the story."

"Oh, yeah, sure," I say. I know how to call a girl. I've done that before.

"Can you call me tonight?"

"Tonight? But . . . I, ah, don't have your number."

"Here." She pulls a notebook out of my bag. Scribbles her number in it. Closes the notebook. And slides it back in the bag.

She looks up at me. Her face is so close I can smell her skin and hair. I don't say anything. I don't even close my eyes. It takes all of my concentration just to stand there and not fall down.

"Talk to you tonight," she says. And then she's gone.

Running down the sidewalk to the car. I stand there holding the book bag. I see a door open. Then I hear it close. I even think I see her wave. I sort of wave back. Not sure if I'm supposed to or not. Then I watch the bus lighting up the whole empty parking lot. Before it disappears around the main classroom building. And I'm still standing there. Holding on to the bag like it's holding me up or something.

• 10 •

Every Friday night my parents go out. Without fail. And I'm left with feeding the kids. Cleaning up. Getting them to bed. I usually make them cheeseburgers. Big and flat like Wendy's. And I don't cook them so they're dried out. Just a couple of minutes on one side. Then I flip them over. Slap on a piece of cheese. Let it melt. Then slide it onto a fresh bun. The kids call them MacWendy's. They can call them whatever they want. Just so long as they eat them.

I shut the cupboard door and turn off the kitchen light. The kids are upstairs playing cars and Legos. I walk into the living room. Check the fire in the Fisher stove. Then walk across the room to my dad's aquarium. The two angels had their eye on me the minute I walked into the room. I can feel their eyes. I open the top. And they poke their noses into the air to show me how hungry they are. A male guppy circles underneath them. His tail flowing like a Chinese kite. I sprinkle a pinch of fish food across the water. The angels attack it. The other fish wait for it to drift down to them.

I sit down in a wooden chair and watch them feed. Thinking, did she really ask me to call her? I stare at the aquarium like it's a crystal ball or something. But it doesn't have any answers. Only a glassfish nibbling on a fat flake. What I can't believe is that she even talked to me! I close my eyes and try to remember what she said. But it's kind of hard to remember something you don't believe. All I remember is the V.W. bus driving off. And walking into the locker room. With the floor all covered with dirty socks and wet towels.

When I walk into the shower steam's billowing into the locker room. And everyone's finished, except for Woody and Brook. Woody's at one end of the shower room. His back to the shower. Brook's at the other. I take a middle shower. Spin the tap and step into the hot spray.

"Where the hell you been, showboat?"

"What?" I look at Woody through the steam like I didn't hear him.

"I said, where the hell you been?"

"Getting my books." I squint through the steam at him.

"You must have a hell of a lot of books," Brook laughs from the other end of the room.

"Shut up, pencil face," Woody shouts. He throws a piece of soap at him. Then, looking at me, "Takes you twenty minutes to get your damn books?"

"Depends." I lean my head back until the shower feels like a warm cap.

"Depends on what?" Woody sounds closer. When I look at him I can see he's taken a couple of steps towards me. I turn and stare at the green tile on the wall. And don't say anything. He's too close and too naked to talk to.

"I said, depends on what?" he shouts.

"You don't have to shout, Woody," Brook says, and turns off his shower and leaves. His feet sound like fish flapping on the wet tile.

"Shut up, Brook. I'll shout if I want to," Woody shouts after him. Then slowly he backs up into his shower. I watch the water spilling down off my forehead. Pretending none of this is happening.

"Depends on what, Mac?" Woody finally asks again.

This time I answer him. "Depends if I'm talking with somebody."

"Yeah? Talking with who?" I can feel his eyes. Just like the angelfish. Staring at me.

"Just somebody."

"Yeah. Well, that somebody just happens to be my girl," he snarls at me.

"Yeah?" I turn off the shower. Walk out of the room. Grab a towel and wrap it around my waist. "Who says?" I call back.

"Who says?" Woody's suddenly standing in the door. Steam rising off his pink skin like he's a dragon or something. "I says," he hisses at me. "Who the hell do you think she's going out with tonight?"

I turn and start for my locker.

"Me!" he shouts. "That's who. So get smart, Mac. You hear me! Next time you talk to her you're dead meat."

When I go upstairs the twins are lying on the rug in their pajamas. Surrounded by Legos shaped like spaceships.

"What are you guys playing?" I kneel down next to Avery. He's the smaller of the twins. He's got straight hair and blue eyes.

"Star Wars," he mumbles to me as he checks out his equipment.

"Star Wars? You've got to be kidding."

"Why?" Peter looks up from his huge construction. His hair is curly. He looks two years older than Avery.

"Don't you guys get tired of that crap?"

"No." Peter shakes his head. Like he could care what I think about his answer.

"You guys." I shake my head to show them I don't approve. But no one notices. So I grab Avery and flip him over my back. Just to show them that there are other things we could be doing.

"Cut it out, Mac." He spins off my shoulders and karates me on the back of my neck. I fall towards Peter. Laughing. Next thing I know they're both on me. Pounding on my back. And Peter is yelling in my ear.

"Mac! Move . . . you're messing up my death star."

It's late. Nearly eleven o'clock. And I just got the guys to bed. I lie on my parents' bed. Their down comforter pulled up to my chin. Their white phone on my chest. I'm holding a scrap of paper with a telephone number written on it in light blue ink. I've been looking at it for a while. Thinking lots of things. Like, what if she's not there when I call? What am I supposed to say? I dial the number with the phone still on the hook. Wishing it would ring on its own. It does. It vibrates right through my ribs to my spine. I pick up the receiver. My hand is shaking.

"Hello?"

"Mac."

"Who's this?"

"We're having a party."

"Who?" I can feel my face beginning to sweat.

"Wanna get high?" the voice slurs.

"Who's this?" I sit up. "Pogo, is this you?"

"Not 'xactly. Not 'xactly."

"Woody?"

"Bingo. Give de man a joint."

"Where are you? Pogo's?"

"Bingo. Give de man anuda joint. Hol' it a minit. Shuddup, you guys. Now where was I?"

"Pogo's."

" 'Xactly. Ya wanna say hi ta Jenny? We been dancing all night. Cheek ta cheek. But I know how much ya like ta talk to her. Lemme get her." I hear him call her. I shiver a little. And pull the comforter up towards my chin. There's a lot of shouting and laughing and music. Finally Woody comes back on the phone.

"Mac?" he shouts.

"Yeah?"

33

"Forget it. She doesn't wanna talk to ya. Ya bore her." I start to hang up, but don't.

"Mac?" his voice gurgles.

"What?" I whisper.

"Mac?"

"I said, what?" I shout at him.

"We're gonna go dance. Okay? No. She says no. Hold it, Mac." I can hear his hand cupping the phone. Then his voice again. "I was wrong, Mac."

"About what?" I ask. Wishing I had never answered the phone.

"She doesn't wanna dance wid me."

"Can you blame her?" I mumble.

"No." He breathes heavily into the phone. "She wants ta go upstairs instead. And do some heavy petting."

"Woody."

" 'Night, dial tone. Jenny sends her best." He hangs up. And the room is quiet again. Like he never called. I crumple up the piece of paper and throw it across the room. Then look at the clock. It's eleven-ten. I drop the phone on the floor. Turn off the light. And stare into the darkness. Wishing I was bigger or he was smaller. So I could strangle the bastard.

• 13 •

I wake up to the phone ringing. I look around the dark room. Trying to figure out where I am. On the night table the red digits of the clock stare at me like eyes. I try and concentrate on the numbers and the ringing. It's eleven-thirty. I must have fallen asleep. I lean over the edge of the bed to answer the phone. But as soon as I touch the cold plastic handle, I stop.

I may be no genius, but I'm not dumb enough to get burned twice. Who else is it but Woody? And there's no way I'm gonna talk to him again. I pick up the receiver and drop it. The phone stops ringing. I roll back onto the bed with a big smile on my face.

I feel pretty good about myself until I start thinking about my parents. Stuff like car accidents, state police, ambulances, and hospitals trying to call to let me know how they are. Were they trying to call? How are they? Have they been in an accident? Are they okay? Are they dead? Or just badly hurt? I sit up, turn on the light, and stare at the wall. Thinking what a jerk I am when the phone rings again. I nearly fall out of bed grabbing the receiver.

"Hello," I answer. "Who's this?"

"Mac?" a voice I can hardly hear whispers.

"Speak louder," I say. "Who is this?"

"Me."

"Who's me? Mum? Is that you?"

"It's not Mum, you dummy. It's me. Jenny."

"Jenny?" What is she calling for? All I can think about is car accidents and Pogo's party. Maybe she got hurt on the way home. "You okay?" I ask.

"I'm fine." Her voice is still a whisper. I have to press the phone hard against my ear to hear her. "You never called," she whispers.

"Oh, I was, ah . . ." I don't know what to say. I try and

listen for the partying in the background. But I hear nothing.

"Probably watching TV, right?" Her voice is as soft as a pillow.

"I, ah, fell asleep."

"Did I wake you?"

"No," I lie.

"You were going to finish your story."

"What story?" I ask.

"About your kid brothers."

"Oh," I mumble. I don't know what's going on with this girl. One minute she's off partying with Woody. The next minute she's calling me up about my kid brothers. "You really want to hear about them?" I ask.

"Yeah," she says. And more quietly, "I just like to hear you tell stories."

"Yeah." I sit up straight and clear my throat. Now I remember. She thinks they're cute and funny. I try and think of cute and funny. That's a long time ago. I start telling her about the first thing that comes to mind. "You really want to hear about those brats?"

"They're not brats."

"Yeah? You don't think so? Well, once when they were two or three, Dad put them down for their nap. You know, in their room and everything. Now, these guys were not your ordinary two year olds. I mean they were so bad that when they took a nap we had to lock them in their room. Otherwise they were all over the house. Raising hell and everything. So you know those hook-and-eye locks?"

"Yeah."

"Well, we had one of those on the door. So anyway, Dad put them down for their nap. Locked them in and everything. Then he went and started doing some project. About an hour or so later he hears water running in the kitchen. He doesn't know what it could be. Mum's at work. I'm at school. The twins are asleep. Right? Wrong. The twins figured out how to unhook the lock."

"How'd they do that?"

"With a Mr. Rogers burglary kit." I stop to listen to her laugh. It's the nicest sound I've heard in my whole life. "I don't know. Maybe Dad didn't lock it. Anyhow, he hears this water running in the kitchen. I mean going full blast. So he comes down the stairs. Real softly. He doesn't know what to expect. Maybe a robber washing some dirty dishes before he steals them. Or a broken pipe. So he tiptoes into the kitchen. Ready for the worst. And boy did he find the worst." I stop talking to take a breath.

"He found the twins, right?"

"Yeah, he found the twins. And a hell of a lot more."

"They were playing in the water?"

"You'll see. So he sneaks into the kitchen. And there are the twins all right. On the loose. Going wild. Both sitting on the counter. Naked except for diapers. One of them has the big flour jar between his legs. The top's off and he's got a wooden scoop in his hand. And he's reaching into the flour jar, taking huge scoops of flour and throwing it across the room. Like he's trying to make the kitchen white or something. And he's completely white himself. From head to foot."

"I don't believe it."

37

"You don't believe it? My father didn't believe it."

"So what did he do? And what about the water?"

"That's the worst of it. The other twin is sitting in the sink. Water running full blast between his legs. And he's got the sprayer, you know, one of those sprayers?"

"For rinsing things?"

"Yeah. Well, he's got this sprayer in his hands. And as fast as one can throw the flour on the floor, the other's hosing it down. And you know what flour and water make?"

"Glue."

"That's right."

"Oh, no," she laughs.

"So what did your father do?"

"He just stood there and said, Bad babies. No, babies. Bad babies."

"Where was your mother?"

"My mother is one smart lady. She's a lawyer. And as soon as the twins were born, she decided it was time to practice law."

"So who takes care of the twins?"

"My dad."

"That's crazy."

"I don't know. He's kind of a crazy guy."

"What do you mean?"

"I mean, he does crazy things all the time. I mean, he does really crazy things. Like at night, when I'm supposed to have my lights off?"

"Yeah." She's already laughing and I haven't even told the story yet.

"Well, my room's on the third floor. Kind of in a little dormer, you know? The only room up there. The only way you can get to it is on a ladder from the playroom. It's kind of a pain for old folks like my parents. So it's real private. Kind of like being on a boat with lots of windows. Anyway. One night Dad calls up and says, Lights out, the way fathers do. Usually if I ignore him he forgets about me and goes away. Anyway, this night he sneaks down into the basement and turns off the circuit breaker to my room. Pretty funny, huh?"

"Yeah." She laughs so I go on.

"Except it totally screws up my alarm clock. And a tape. 'Cause the fact is, I was in the middle of taping Casey Kasem's Top Forty."

"So what did you do?"

"I yelled at him."

"What did he do?"

"Went to sleep."

She laughs pretty hard.

"You think that's bad? Another night I'm lying in bed reading when there's a knock on my window. I look up and there's this burglar with a stocking over his head, trying to break in to my room."

"What did you do? Were you scared?"

"Was I scared? Of course I wasn't scared. I just jumped off my bed and went leaping out of my room without touching the ladder. That's an eight-foot drop. Luckily I don't remember landing. Just running into my parents' room shouting, Burglar! There's a burglar in my room! My mother puts down the magazine she's reading and stares at me. Then I notice Dad's not in bed. Where's Dad? I shout. Where's Dad? There's a burglar in my room! And she says, He's climbing up the side of the house, dear. To spray the hornets' nest under your eaves. Hornets' nest? I shout. Yes, dear. And he put one of my old stockings over his head so he wouldn't get stung." Jenny's laughing so hard I just sit there. Resting the phone on my shoulder. When she stops I begin again.

"You know what's worse than hornets?" I ask. "According to the twins."

"What?"

"Thornets."

"Thornets?"

"Yeah. Thornets are deadly. They have thorns for stingers and . . ."

"You're making it up." She laughs even louder now.

"Am not. Anyway Dad loves to tell that story. How when he tried to get my attention to open the window all I did was howl. And then leap out of the room."

"You could have been killed."

"That's what I say."

"What did he say?"

"That he was sorry. It was a mistake. But I don't know. I think he probably thought to himself all along, We'll just give Mac a little scare. He really is crazy."

We talk for hours. Or so it seems. I don't know about what. And I don't care. Just talking to her and hearing her voice makes me the happiest kid on this planet. Like I just won the lottery or something. When we finally hang up I just sit there staring at the wall. Feeling both happy and confused. Wondering, How can this girl go out with Woody and spend so much time talking with me?

• 14 •

I stand in front of the mirror that hangs on the closet door. And stare at myself. Who the hell would like a kid that looks like that? I wonder. Baby blond curls. Fat cheeks. And skinny. Sort of. I try to make a muscle with my right arm. But I have to press behind it with my left hand to make something of it. I'm thinking, well, that's pathetic, when the phone rings for the third time that night.

"Hello," I answer. "Who's this?"

"It's me."

"Jenny?"

"I forgot to ask you something." Her voice is like ice cream.

"Me?" What does she want to ask me?

"You going to . . . you know . . . the dance at school?"

"What dance?"

"Next month."

"I don't know." How do I know?

"Will you go with me?"

Me? I say the word to myself, like I never heard it before. Me? Can she mean me? She can't mean me. She can't mean the dance.

"You mean the dance at the ski lodge?" I ask.

"Yes." Her voice is trembling.

41

"I thought you'd go, you know, ah, with somebody else."

"Like who?"

"I don't know. Somebody like Woody, I guess."

"Who's Woody?"

"Who's Woody?" I can't believe her. "He's the guy you went out with tonight."

"I didn't go out with any guy tonight!" She's not whispering anymore.

"You didn't?"

"No! I didn't!"

"But I thought . . ." Finally my mind catches up to my mouth. My friend Woody has been lying through his teeth. So what else is new?

"You thought I went out with some jerk I don't even know?"

"I guess he lied and I believed him." I'm feeling kind of like a jerk myself. "It was my mistake."

"Your mistake? It was his mistake. Who is this guy?"

"Woody? Who's Woody?" I can't believe her question. But I answer it anyway. "He's the big guy on the soccer team? Who told all the funny jokes?"

"That jerk?"

"Yeah. That jerk." I can't believe she's calling Woody a jerk.

"Who the hell does he think he is?"

"I don't know."

"Yeah, well, he's a creep. Just like all the other macho creeps who lie about me. I'm so sick of them. Saying I'm going out with them or doing things with them. When I don't even know them. I hate them. I hate all of them."

Suddenly she's crying. And I don't know what to do or say. I just hold on to the phone and listen. Hoping she doesn't think I'm like any of those creeps. Thinking maybe I should hang up and leave her alone. But I don't. I just listen and keep saying I'm sorry. Until finally she stops crying.

"It gets me so angry," she says through the last tears.

"Yeah. All those jerks trying to get you to do things you don't want to do," I say. And then, out of nowhere, "That reminds me."

"Of what?"

"Never mind. It's stupid."

"Of what, Mac?"

"Just of jerks making you do things you don't want to."

"Like what?"

"Like physicals. They're making me take a physical for soccer."

"Yuck. I hate physicals. They're dumb."

"You're not kidding."

And then, in a voice so weird I hardly recognize it, she says, "Take off your clothes, please." It sounds so funny and so strange that I laugh until I have tears in my eyes.

When I finally stop, she asks, "So after all that ... do you want to go with me ... to the dance?"

"Do you want to go with me?" is all I can say.

"Why do you think I called, you dummy?"

I don't know. I'm too stupid to know why you called.

But what difference does that make? I've never let stupidity get in my way before. So, as calmly as I can, I say, "Yes, I'll go to the dance with you." A hundred times yes.

• 15 •

The dance is upstairs. I climb the stairway. Slowly. Wondering if I'm wearing the right thing. Gray pants and a red shirt. The music is so loud the stairs are vibrating. At the top of the landing I stop and wait for my eyes to get adjusted. It's dark. Except for the light show. Flashing on and off in the middle of the room.

A bunch of eleventh-grade kids are already dancing. I walk slowly towards the table where there's a punch bowl and junk food. I don't see her anywhere. The song changes. A chain of girls nearly run me over getting to the dance floor. They all dance with big smiles on their faces. Like they're on MTV. I walk over to the punch bowl and pick up a plastic cup.

Woody, Brook, and Shawn are standing behind the table. Crumbs on their faces. Plastic cups of punch in their hands.

"There he is," Woody shouts across the punch bowl at me. "God's gift to women."

"Shut up, Woody."

"Speaking of women, where is she?"

"Who?" Why do the wrong words always come out of my mouth at the wrong time? I know who he's talking about. Everyone does. I should say something like, Stay-

44

ing miles away from you, buddy. But I don't. I just say, who.

"Who? Who? What are you, an owl?" Woody shakes his head. "Or a pigeon?" And then, pretending to talk to Shawn, "To think that a girl would waste her time on such a nerd. There must be something wrong with her."

"Obviously." Shawn nods his head like he's agreeing. But he winks at me. Like a jerk I wink back.

"She's probably got plastic breasts. Or some other defect. But Mac wouldn't know anything about that. Would you, Mac?"

"Shut up, Woody. You don't have to be a total ass. Just try being what you are. Half-ass."

"Oh, brilliance. Such brilliance. I've been shot with brilliance." He staggers back against a window.

"There she is," Brook interrupts. He nods towards the top of the stairs.

"Who?" I cluck like a dumb bird.

"Your girl, you idiot. The one with the plastic tits," Woody hisses at me through the music.

"Woody! I already told you to shut up." When I turn around I see her standing at the head of the stairs. She's wearing a white shirt. A shell necklace. And her hair looks blacker. Her face more beautiful than I remember. I just stand there. And stare at her.

Shawn is slapping me on the back. Woody is saying something dirty. I can tell by his voice. I've got to get away from these jerks. And the next thing I know I'm walking towards her. Concentrating on not falling down.

On not losing my breath. I'm nearly halfway there when she turns and sees me. She smiles. My heart stops.

"Hi." Just like that she's standing in front of me.

"Hi," I say. My heart starts beating again.

"I like your shirt." She reaches out and touches it. "It's Hawaiian." Embarrassed, I look away and see Woody and Shawn walking towards us. I take her hand and walk out onto the dance floor. Just to get away from them.

"Want to dance?" I ask when we stop under the mirrored light. She doesn't answer but puts her left hand on my shoulder. I put my right hand around her waist. I can feel her spine against my fingers! And we begin to dance to the music.

"Is my shirt okay?" she asks, looking up at me.

"What do you mean?" I look at her. Her eyes no more than three inches from my own. All I can see are her eyes and eyelashes. Her cheeks and her lips. I can even smell her hair and skin.

"This shirt's kind of baggy. It was my dad's. It's supposed to be baggy."

"I like it," I say.

"It's not too baggy?"

"No. It's perfect."

"Oh, good." She rests her head against my shoulder and closes her eyes. "You're such a good guy, Mac."

I don't say anything. I think I should pull her tightly to me. But I don't. I just continue to dance. Trying not to notice that her hair is making my chin itch. We dance like that until the song ends. Then we dance fast. We don't even leave the dance floor for punch. We just dance.

Towards the last set when we're sweaty, all they play are slow ones. And we dance close. So close I can't tell who's moving whose legs. Her face is pressed against my neck. I've never felt such smooth skin. And all I want to do is kiss her. But I don't. I just close my eyes. And dance.

"Excuse me." Someone bumps into me from behind.

"Sorry." I turn to get out of the way. But we bump again. I turn around to see who it is. It's Woody and Shawn dancing like bumper cars. They go flying past us. Woody has his eyes closed. And Shawn has his head tucked into Woody's shoulder.

"Darling," Woody moans.

"Darling," Shawn echoes.

"This is it."

"Hold me tight." They disappear down the dance floor.

"Let's get out of here." Jenny grabs my hand and pulls me towards the stairs. "Let's take a walk."

Outside, the sky is splattered with stars. We walk up the T-bar slope away from the lodge. Away from the music and lights. The air is cool and fresh. We climb up the slope until we can see the lights of Cummington across the river. Then we sit down. Out of breath. This is where I ski all winter. It's not a big mountain. But it's fun. I tell Jenny what my favorite trails are.

She pulls her coat tight around her. I zip my vest closed. Over by the Hoosic Range a train whistles. We sit there on the slope and listen. Now we can hear the throbbing of the diesel engines. It's coming this way. Getting louder and louder. Pretty soon we can't even hear the music at all.

Jenny leans against me. To keep from falling over I put

47

my arm around her. She looks up at me. We're so close to each other I'm breathing her air. And all I can see are her lips. I touch them with mine. She puts a hand around my neck and pulls me against her. Pressing our lips together. And just like that we're kissing! And I don't ever want to stop kissing. Because if we do I might die.

And the train rumbles by. So close and so loud the whole mountain is shaking.

• 16 •

The nurse is a short, fat woman who sticks out in front just as much as she sticks out in back. She keeps adjusting the form on her clipboard. Nodding her head up and down so that her double chin folds and unfolds. She's wearing a black nametag clipped to her white collar. And if I were real close to her I could read her name. But I'm not.

She's dressed all in white the way nurses are. With white tights and white shoes. She asks me if I had some twenty different diseases I have never heard of. And if I have allergies. She leads me out of the waiting room. Down a long, dark corridor to an examination room. Her shoes squeak on the dark linoleum like she's walking on mice or something.

"Undress and Doctor will be with you in a minute," she says, as she reaches over the examination table. And pulls a fat sheet of white paper down over a skinny little mattress. I don't say anything, but wait for her to leave the room. She squeaks across the floor and closes the door behind her. I listen to her squeaking back up the hallway and then I look around the examination room. Wishing I were with Jenny. Or anyplace. But here.

The walls are some dirty color I've never seen before. The ceiling is the same dirty color. And in the middle is a flat circle of white light. I climb up on the examination table and the paper crinkles under me. Slick and smooth under my palms. Like butcher paper. There's a glass cabinet in the corner filled with all kinds of stainless steel things on paper towels. Next to the cabinet is a scale. In the other corner of the room is a little white sink with a mirror over it. I'm just about to get up and look at my face when the doctor walks in.

He's wearing a white jacket and carrying a folder. He closes the door behind him and locks it. Then he tries turning the doorknob to make sure it doesn't move.

"Well, well." He looks up and seems surprised to see me sitting there. "So, you're Mac. Of course you are." He's wearing brown glasses. His thin black hair is combed from his left ear all the way over his bald head to his right ear.

"So, you're Mac?" he repeats, as he puts the folder down at the end of the examination table. This time I feel like I'm supposed to answer.

"Yes." I nod my head the way I think you're supposed to nod your head to a doctor. Only he doesn't even see me. He's studying the form the nurse filled out and mumbling to himself. Like he doesn't have enough time for all this. I wish he didn't. I wish I was someplace else. Anyplace else. Physicals are so dumb. Like I'm about to die tomorrow or something.

"Now, let me see." He looks up from the folder. His

forehead and cheeks are red. "Hot in here, isn't it?"

I think it's cold, but I'm just a kid. Who am I to argue with a doctor?

"We keep it that way on purpose. So no one catches a cold. Now, tell me, aren't you the goalie for the Cummington soccer team, Mac?"

I nod.

"Yes, yes. I thought so. My daughter went to Swift River. And I still go to all of their athletic events. So I've seen you play, you know." I relax a little. Thinking maybe he's all right. He steps in front of me and stares at me, his eyes black lights. I turn away.

"Yes, you're very good, Mac." He puts his hands on my shoulders and begins to tap the upper part of my back.

"Thank you, Doctor," I hear myself answering.

"Call me Paul. After all, I was a kid once myself."

I look down at the floor.

"Yes, you're quite an athlete. It surprises me, quite frankly, because you're so beautifully delicate."

My mouth is dry. I don't believe what he said. I can feel my face turning red.

"I haven't embarrassed you, have I?"

"No," I lie.

"Good." He stops tapping me on the back and steps away. "Well, now, let's get on with this. Just undress and I'll examine you."

"To my underpants?"

"Goodness no, Mac. Take everything off. I need to see all of you."

· TWO ·

17

It's nearly two months since the dance. I hardly see Jenny anymore. Except tonight. It's January. Snow's on the ground. Haven't skied yet. Haven't even gone out for the team.

We're sitting in one of those booths. Me and Jenny. At Shelburne Pizza. Trying to talk over the plastic tabletop. But the place is so crowded and the juke box is so loud. We can't hear each other. So we just eat the pizza. Hardly saying a word. By the time we get to the last piece it's cold. The cheese is like rubber. I try drilling holes through it with a straw. But the straw keeps bending. She touches my hand like it's an accident. Her fingers cold as a can of Coke. I pull my hand away.

"What's wrong?" she asks.

"Nothing," I shrug. I can feel a burning where her fingers touched my skin. "Let's get out of here." I stand up and pull on my parka. "It's too loud in here."

She follows me out the glass door into the cold. Our breath white in the streetlight. It's cold. January cold. And it's beginning to snow. I zip up my coat. She pulls up her collar. We walk between the parked cars, across the street to the bridge. Halfway across we stop and stare down at the river. It's black and spotted with lights.

"Going to jump?" she jokes.

I don't answer. Just stand there. Staring at the dark water. Wondering how cold it would be. How long it'd take to hit bottom. And if I'd break any bones.

"Come on," she says after a while. "It's getting cold. I want to go home."

She tugs the sleeve of my parka. We start walking. Tiny specks of snow are swirling out of the streetlights into our faces. We walk up past the bank, the drugstore, and the library. We don't say anything until we're up to the Chevy dealer. We stop and look in through the plate glass window at a black Z-28. Just sitting there. Waiting for some kid to take off in it. I think of all the places I'd go if I ever got a Z-28. Brook's always talking about Mexico. I wouldn't have to go that far. California would be fine.

"If you could go anywhere you wanted," I ask her reflection in the window, "where would you go?"

"Home."

"I mean, if you had a Z-28?"

"Home. I'm cold." She starts up the hill.

"I mean, if you had a Z-28 and a credit card. Where would you go?"

"I'd drive home. Come on." She disappears into the shadow of a tree outside the nursing home. Where there are no streetlights. And it's dark except for the glow of television sets and night lights.

"I'd rather be dead than live in a nursing home," I mumble, as we cut across the street on an angle. She doesn't answer.

I follow her down the sidewalk. Past houses with snow blowing like curtains through their porch lights. Thinking about old people and broken bones and Z-28s racing down the highway out of control.

"Remember that accident last month?" I don't know if I'm thinking or talking. Until I hear my voice, like an echo, come back to me. "On the highway? You remember? By the church?"

She doesn't answer. I keep talking. "Only a couple of miles from your house. Remember? All across the road. Ripped fenders. Pieces of engines. Glass. Shattered everywhere. Like ice."

"Why are you talking about this?" She stops and turns on me, her voice angry.

"I don't know. I just remember."

"Well, I don't want to remember." And she starts walking again. Away from me across somebody's lawn. "Why should I want to remember something like that?"

I don't say anything. But I follow her across the lawn. There's no sound except our boots squeaking through the new snow. I don't want to remember either. But I do. All of us in the school bus. Coming home from I don't know where. And there in the middle of the road, glass and bent metal everywhere. And an arm. A real arm in a real sleeve. Lying across the double yellow line. And the hand. Pointing towards the neon sign in front of the Baptist Church that says, SINNERS WAIT FOR THE 11TH HOUR. OUR SERVICE BEGINS AT 10:30.

I want to ask Jenny about the arm in the road. Was it really there? Pointing to the sign? Or am I just making it up?

18

She cuts across a driveway towards the back of a house. A big white Victorian. I follow her up the back steps onto a cold porch. It's my first time to her house. We take off our boots and coats. Then carry them into the kitchen. She drops her stuff on a chair. I dump mine on top. It's a big kitchen with red counters and white cupboards. A stove but no icebox.

"Where's the icebox?" I ask.

"In the cellar. Mom's on a diet."

"All these moms on diets."

"She says if she's going to eat anything, she'll have to work for it."

"What about your dad?"

"He doesn't live here."

"I don't blame him."

"Mac, I told you they're divorced. And it has nothing to do with the icebox."

"I'm sorry. It was just a joke." I follow her down the cellar stairs. It's a real creepy cellar. She takes two cans of Diet Coke out of the icebox and hands me one. Then we go up to the library and turn on the television. Where it's as cold as the back porch. I leave the room and come back with our parkas. She pulls hers over her shoulders. I zip mine shut. Being cold isn't worth the aggravation. I'd rather haul wood all summer for my father than be cold in the winter. Jenny gets up from her seat, goes over to a big wooden chest, and pulls out a blanket. She sits down next to me and spreads it over our legs.

"Where's your mum?" I ask, as the blanket settles around us.

"Don't know." She pulls the blanket up to her chin.

The TV has lousy reception. The voices are fuzzy and the picture blinks. It's a pain to watch. But I don't say anything. I take my Coke out from underneath the blanket and take a sip. Jenny reaches over. Pulls the can from me. Takes a sip and puts it down on the floor next to hers. I don't move. Even when she leans towards me and her lips are next to mine I don't move. She says something. But I can't hear her. It's like she's so close to me she's a thousand miles away. I should kiss her, I think. She wants me to kiss her. But I don't. I don't do anything.

"You ever have bad dreams?" I ask, instead of kissing her.

"What?" She leans her head back so that she can see me. "What did you ask?"

"If you ever had bad dreams." I look away from her face, across the room at the empty bookshelves. "You know, bad dreams."

"Of course. Who hasn't?"

"I mean one dream over and over again."

"Yeah? So?"

"I don't know. I mean, I've been . . . kind of having this one dream over and over."

"So?" Her voice is angry. She pushes away from me. Leans back into the couch and looks down at the blanket wrapped tight around our legs. Then she looks back at me. I look down at the blanket. I can feel her eyes on my forehead.

"So what's the dream?" Her voice is gentler now.

"Weird," I mumble under my breath. Wondering, What am I doing talking to her about dreams?

"Dreams usually are weird." And then she doesn't say anything and there's just the noise of the television. And her sitting next to me waiting to hear my dream. I start talking.

"I keep dreaming about this one room. Like a doctor's room, you know? With all that stuff. Like an examination table and a scale to get weighed on and shelves filled with different colored bottles." I glance up at her to see if she's listening. She is. I pull the blanket up to my chin and continue.

"I'm lying on the table looking at the ceiling. It has those white squares dotted with little black holes." Why do I remember the black holes? "And then there's this light like a face staring down at me."

"What do you mean, like a face?"

"I don't know." I can feel tiny drops of sweat beading around my lips.

"So then what?"

"Then —" I'm leaning on my left wrist and my hand's gone to sleep. I shake it. Blood rushes through my wrist. "Then the walls start collapsing."

"Like an earthquake, you mean?"

"No. Like a horror movie, they start sliding in. And the

ceiling and the light start pressing down on me. The room gets smaller and smaller —"

"Like a coffin?"

"Until I can't breathe."

"Then what?"

"Then I wake up."

"I don't like that dream. That's a nightmare, not a dream, and it gives me the creeps." She stands up and leaves the room. When she comes back she's carrying a glass of cider. She hands it to me. Picks up the blanket. Throws it up over her head. And sits down next to me. The blanket settles down around us. She smiles. I try and smile back. She takes the glass out of my hand. Takes a sip and then gently holds the cold glass against my cheek. It makes me feel like I have a black eye or something. I stare through the glass at her. I can tell she thinks I'm feeling better. Just by the way she's looking at me.

She puts the glass on the floor next to the empty cans and puts her cold hand up to my face. Then she leans towards me until her mouth is touching my lips. She closes her eyes. I close mine. Then I feel her mouth open and her tongue pushing gently against my lips. I look at the TV out of the corner of my eye. And sit there with her tongue in my mouth. Wondering how long it'll be until my ride comes.

19

I lie in bed and stare at the track lights in the dark. My head aches. My teeth are sore. I pull a pillow over my head and wait for the alarm to go off. I'm freezing cold. Must be zero out there. And the wind. That's what woke me. Howling hard enough to blow the roof off. I pull the blankets up over my head.

The alarm goes off. Every morning. Like clockwork. I look up from under the pillows and squint at the red digits glaring at me. Six-thirty. Then I pound the sleep button. The alarm shuts off. Next time I'll mangle it. I lie there waiting for it to dare buzz me one more time. I feel a pimple pushing against my chin. I rub my fingers over the swelling. God, how I hate waking up in the morning.

"Mac? You up?" Somewhere from the pit of the house I hear my dad calling.

"No!" I shout back.

"Good. No school today." No school today. Such a brilliant joke. Such a brilliant humorist. Every morning of my life I hear the same stupid joke. Every morning of my life. No school today. A regular riot. I kick the covers off my feet and roll out of bed. In another couple of months I'll be bigger than him and I'm gonna knock his ass across the room. No school today? Hah, hah, hah. What a riot. How about a ride across the room? Bam! Slap him up against the wall. Not so funny, every morning, is it? But I don't say anything. I'm a good kid.

I climb down the ladder and stumble into the bathroom. Turn on the shower and stand under the steaming hot spray. I can feel the water soften my brain. Didn't do my homework last night. Forgot all about it. Lying in bed listening to tapes. Gonna get yelled at.

"Mac, what's wrong with you? This isn't like you," Mrs. Miller will nag.

No shit, I'll say.

"You haven't done your homework in weeks."

No shit.

"So what are we going to do about this?"

Try kissing my ass.

But I won't say that. Every day the same questions. And every day I just stand there dumb, and nod my head like I can't talk.

"Are you going to do your work tonight?" they'll all ask.

I'll nod my head.

"Promise?"

I'll nod my head again. But I don't work. I just lie. Lie in bed and listen to tapes. It's the only thing that keeps me from thinking. Listening to tapes through earphones turned up loud enough to blast my brains out. I turn the shower hotter. I like it so hot I can't stand it. So I don't have to think about anything.

"Mac." Someone's always calling me. I put my head further under the shower. It's so hot I can feel my brain shrinking. Right down to the size of a frog's brain.

"Mac, you didn't do your homework."

How can a frog do homework?

"Mac, you didn't do your homework again."

Beedeep . . . beedeep.

"Mac! Breakfast is ready," he's calling from the kitchen.

"Coming, Dad," I croak. Get it, Dad, croak? Only he doesn't hear me. He's listening to some stupid news show. It's always the same. Every morning of my life. I turn off the shower and stand in front of the mirror. The bathroom is filled with mist. The mirror is coated with tiny beads of water. That's how I see myself. Through a fog.

I look for my toothbrush on the counter. No toothbrushes. And what did the little bastards do with them this morning? Every day it's something different. Having little brothers is such a pain. Half the time I'd like to strangle them. So I'm gonna go to school with bad breath just because my little brothers like to hide toothbrushes. I'm not putting up with this. I fling open the door and pound down the hall to their room.

"Little brothers," I shout, as I flip on their overhead light. "Out of bed this minute." They look up at me through squinty eyes. "Now," I shout.

"What for?" the one in the top bunk squeaks. I grab him by his pajama top and yank him out of bed. Then I grab the other one and shove them both into the bathroom.

"Okay, squirts, where're the toothbrushes?" They stare at me like I'm speaking a foreign language. Then Peter points to the floor. And there, strewn across the tile next to the toilet, are the toothbrushes.

"Terrific," I shout.

"They fell," Avery whimpers.

"Toothbrushes don't fall!" I reach down and grab the brushes. They're wet. I hold them up and sniff them. They stink.

"Mother," I shout. The twins bolt from the bathroom. "Mother!" I shout again.

"What?" she answers from her bedroom.

"The twins pissed on my toothbrush."

"They what?"

"They pissed on the toothbrushes," I shout at the top of my lungs.

But she doesn't hear me. Because the smoke detector outside the bathroom just went off. And it sounds just like the end of the world. Just like a dying pterodactyl. Coming crashing down on my head.

"What the hell," my father says, lunging up the stairs, "is going on?"

"Fire alarm," I shout.

"No kidding," he shouts back at me. At times like this, my dad has such a way with words. He quickly smells the air. Not a trace of smoke. He grabs a towel and holds it over the alarm.

"Idiot," he growls.

I don't wait around to hear the rest. I don't need his crap. It's the same old story. I took too long of a shower. The fact that the alarm can't tell the difference between steam from a shower and smoke from a fire doesn't mean a thing. I'm the jerk. Of course no one's gonna say anything about the precious twins pissing on the toothbrushes. Hell, no. Save all the crap for Mac.

20

I sit at the kitchen table pushing scrambled eggs from one side of the plate to the other. It's still dark outside. The house is quiet now. The twins are probably sitting upstairs on their rug staring at their clothes. I rub my chin where the pimple is boring a hole through my skin. I'm not hungry. I can't remember the last time I was. Food makes my stomach turn. I push the plate of eggs across the table and take a sip of orange juice.

"Almost ready?" My mother walks across the kitchen with short steps. The heels of her shoes snap against the wood floor like hammers.

"Yeah." I get up and throw the plate of eggs in the sink.

"Honey, you didn't eat anything." She rushes by me towards the bathroom with eye make-up in her hand. "You feel okay?"

"Yeah." I pick up a brown bag on the counter and drop it on top of my book bag.

"Good. You want to start the car?"

"Yeah." I pull on my parka, grab my book bag, and step outside. The wind snaps through me like I'm a sheet. I jump into the car. Press the accelerator and turn the key. The engine grinds slowly. Like it's filled with mud. Somehow it fires and starts. I move over to the passenger seat and wait. The heater blows cold air against my ankles. I sit there hoping I'll freeze to death. But the odds are against it. I have to go to school to hear the same old thing.

"But, Mac, you promised me you'd do your homework."

What do I tell them today? That I was planning to die so I thought it'd all be a waste of time? They'd like that. My mother gets in the car and next thing I know we're driving down the mountain just like every other morning. Moving past the cold clapboard houses. My mother doesn't say a word. Never does. She just drives. Her blond hair feathered back across her ears. Like an old cover girl.

"You talk to them?" I break the silence.

"Who?"

"The twins."

"About what?"

"About what?" I whisper the words. "About pissing on my toothbrush."

"They didn't really do that, did they, Mac?"

"Nah." I shake my head real slow so she can see me out of the corner of her eye. "Just something I made up."

"You don't have to be nasty."

"I'm not nasty. I'm mad."

"Well, I don't blame you. That's not very good hygiene."

"Mother, you're brilliant."

"Don't be rude." She stares down at me across the blue make-up she's got under her eyes. "I want to change the subject. There's something else we should be talking about, young man."

Oh, no. Young man. Here it comes. The young man lecture. I wonder which one it's going to be. Dirty room? Too long showers? Flunking grades? Rotten attitude?

"Do you think you could use some new clothes?" she asks in her nicest voice.

New clothes? I don't get it. She's got to be up to something. But I can't figure it out. "Sure," I answer slowly. "I could use new clothes. Who couldn't?"

"Good. And it seems you could use some new underwear, too. Is that size still okay for you?"

"What do you mean, new underwear?" What does she know about my underwear?

"Well, I was going through your clothes last night and noticed —"

"What are you doing going through my clothes? I don't go through your clothes, do I?"

"I was doing the laundry, young man."

"Snooping through my clothes!"

"It's not so unusual for a mother to notice her son's clothes when she's doing the laundry. Perhaps you would prefer to wash your own clothes?"

"Yeah, maybe I would, if that's the only way a person can get some privacy around this dump."

"I'm sorry, Mac. I wasn't meaning to invade your privacy. I just want to make sure you have what you need."

"Yeah, well, what I need is a little privacy. And how come you care so much about how I look but you don't care that I have to brush my teeth with a pissed-on toothbrush?"

"Mac, that's enough."

"I don't walk in on you when you're in the shower."

"What does that have to do with anything?"

"Privacy."

"Helping you figure out your clothes?"

"Yes."

"All right. I give up. I'll just stay out of your life. Okay?"

"Good. You just do that!"

I watch her jaw muscles tighten and her hands grip the steering wheel so hard that her fingers turn white. I slouch down in the seat. And stare out the window at the sides of the mountains. They're covered with trees. As ugly as hair on a man's leg.

• 21 •

"What's wrong, Mac?"

"Nothing." It's third period and I'm sitting on the sofa in the principal's office.

"Something's bugging you, Mac. You're not the kind of kid who goes around getting into fights. At least you weren't."

"People can change."

"Sure they can."

"So maybe I've changed."

"So let's talk about it."

"I don't want to talk about it."

"Okay." Mr. Rosen walks around from behind his desk and sits down in a big easy chair across from me. "What do you want to do?"

Even though I'm staring out the window at the mountains I can feel his eyes staring at the back of my head. I turn and stare right back at him. Just to show him I'm not scared. Then I turn back to the window.

"Hmmm?"

"What's the big deal?" I finally answer. "I mean, all I did was punch Shawn after he punched me."

"Yes, that's right." Mr. Rosen looks at me the way he always does to show that he knows exactly what you mean. "Only, Shawn hit you on the shoulder and you hit him in the mouth."

"So?"

"So, for starters, that's not the same thing. And for seconds, that's not like you."

"Yeah? Well, I've been wanting to punch Shawn for a long time."

"Yeah? How come?"

" 'Cause he bugs me."

"So why'd you punch him now?"

"I don't know. It just seemed like a good opportunity."

"Some opportunity, Mac. So what do you think about it now? Now that you're sitting in here talking to the principal about it?"

"I don't know. I still think it was a good idea. I really got him good. I mean, if you're gonna punch somebody, you might as well punch him so he'll remember it."

"Listen, Mac. I think you threw a sucker punch, and I don't think you're the kind of kid who does that kind of thing. There's something else, too."

"What else?" I moan under my breath.

"A couple of your teachers have told me that you've been acting up in class and around the school. I don't know what this is all about, Mac, but I want it to stop. Seventh period today you have a study, right?" I nod.

"Instead of going to study I want you to go see Mr. Cartledge."

"The counselor?"

"That's right."

"What if I don't want to see him?"

"You'll see him."

"Why?"

"Because I'm giving you the chance to figure this thing out, Mac, before we have to do anything drastic to modify your behavior. Now what period do you have? Civics?" I nod.

"Okay, off you go . . . and no more sucker punches, Mac."

"It wasn't a sucker punch."

"Let me make myself clear, Mac. I don't want to hear about any more fights. Period. You got it?"

"Yeah, Mr. Rosen, I got it."

"Good. Well, don't just sit there. Off to class with you."

• 22 •

I never went to civics. Ever since the elections all we've done is talk about the Constitution. I can take a week of it, but two months? I mean, who needs the Bill of Rights to know what your freedoms are? I know my rights. I don't have to do anything I don't want to. So I get my parka and go outside and sit on the back steps. It's cold, but the sun's out and I can look down across the soccer field to the river and across the river to Thunder Mountain where they're making snow.

I like looking across the river at the mountain. It snowed the other night. The fields are filled with snow and the trees down by the river hold snow in their branches like it's a full-time job. Even the rocks and the boulders in the river are white. And the water is silver.

Over on the mountain I can see snow blowing out of the snow guns. And I can hear the snow cats working the snow up on the trails. And the diesel engines of the chair lifts throbbing away in their wooden shacks. I can feel the sun on my back and the cold air on my cheeks. I should feel terrific sitting out here instead of sitting in civics. But I don't. I feel like I want to cry. And punch out everybody at the same time. I'm fighting with everybody. Even Jenny.

"Just adolescence," my dad says. What the hell does he know? And what the hell does that mean? Adolescence?

"Nothing," he tells me, in his smart-ass way. "It just means that you're growing a lot. It just means that you might have a hormone imbalance."

Hormones, I tell him, I don't have hormones. Only women have hormones. So then I get a ten-minute lecture on the wonderful world of hormones. From insulin to testosterone.

"That's the hormone that's giving you so much trouble

right now. That's what makes the hair grow under your arms and . . . and other places."

I hate it when he thinks he's being so open with me about sex. I hate it when he talks about sex with me.

"It's a strong hormone and it makes you aggressive, headstrong, and horny."

Who says I'm horny? I'm not interested in sex. Ask Jenny. I could care less about sex. But what does he know? He could care less.

"That's all I thought about when I was your age."

That's your problem, Dad. Not mine.

"So I know that's what's on your mind."

How do you know what's on my mind?

"So don't worry about it, Mac."

Worry about what?

"These little changes."

I don't want to talk about it.

"I didn't want to talk about it either."

Good for you.

"It's just the way things work."

Good.

"And there's nothing wrong with sex."

Why do all these grown men want to talk to me about sex? Everybody talks about sex. I don't want to talk about sex. I don't want to talk about anything. With anybody. Least of all, Cartledge. Something's wrong with me and nobody cares. Not even my father.

I stare across the white field. Why am I this way? All of the time? And Cartledge. All he'll want to talk about is sex. Why is the world so full of sex maniacs? And why am I sitting here on the back steps of the school? With tears running down my face. It's cold. So cold the tears turn to ice on my cheeks. Oh, God, I hate being this way. I hate it. I'd rather be dead.

• 23 •

Everyone's shouting and stuffing food in their mouths. Like a bunch of jerks. I just sit there and watch them.

"Mac, gimme a bite of your sandwich." It's Brook. Begging for his daily handout.

"Here — take the whole damn thing." I throw a salami sandwich in a plastic bag at him. It bounces off his chin.

"You're such a pain in the ass," he complains.

"You got my sandwich, didn't you? What do you want? Your nose spread across your face like peanut butter?"

"Oh, he's tough. So tough." Woody whistles through his teeth.

"Better watch out, Brook," someone calls from another table.

"I'm scared. Let me tell you," Brook mumbles, as he unwraps the sandwich. "Real scared."

"So what happened to you, Mac?" Woody talks around a fat grinder he's holding with both hands. "What'd Rosen do?"

"Nothing."

"Nothing? After you smashed Shawn in the face?"

"Where is he?"

72

"He went home, you idiot. Or to the clinic. His mouth wouldn't stop bleeding." Woody sinks his teeth into the end of the grinder and yanks his head back. A fistful of cold cuts and lettuce dangles from his mouth. Someone kicks the back of my chair. I turn around and whoever it was is gone. Everyone seems to be talking louder. Voices are flying around the cafeteria like in an insane asylum. I get up to leave.

"Where you going?" someone asks.

"Away." I push through the aisles of chairs. Strewn with books and coats. Kids half standing and half sitting. I haven't eaten anything but I feel sick to my stomach.

"Hey, Mac," I hear somebody call, but I don't look. I just keep walking. There's a kid who jumps up in front of me. I push by him and keep walking.

"He pushed you good," a voice laughs behind me.

"Ego trip," another voice yells.

I'm going to gag. I push through the double exit door. And sprint down the empty corridor. Slam through the men's room door and lean over an empty sink. I stare at bare porcelain but nothing happens. Just empty spasms up and down my throat and spine. My teeth ache. My ears pop. My mouth is full of saliva. But I don't throw up. Slowly the spasms stop. I spit in the sink. Pour water on my face. And begin to breathe again. I punch the blower on the wall and step into the warm stream of air. I can feel it tightening the skin around my face. Like a mask. I'm getting ready to see the counselor.

73

24

"Sit down, sit down." He's standing at a bookshelf with a book in his hand. A smile smeared across his face like eye make-up.

"So, you're Mac." He says it like he's never seen a kid before.

"That's right." I sit down on the couch.

"That's right. Sit down, Mac. Make yourself comfortable."

"Sure," I mumble to myself. I bet he's always looking for a book when he knows someone's coming in. It goes with his smile. I look around the office. One wall is a blackboard and the other wall is lined with green metal bookcases and a green file cabinet. There's a big window at the end of the room that looks up towards the mountain. His desk is facing away from the window.

"Be right with you." I watch him flip open to the front of the book and stand there like he's just made a great discovery or something. He's not a big man. About my height. But his stomach stretches his purple sweater out like it's a balloon. So he can't button his green sports jacket. He keeps nodding his half-bald head.

"Well," he mumbles. "Well." He looks up from his book, puts it back in the shelf, pushes his lips together like he's blowing smoke, then sits down in the chair across from me.

"Very, very interesting."

"What?" I hear myself asking.

"I understand that you like sports."

"Sort of."

"You play soccer and ski?"

"So?"

"So." He pinches his lips between his thumb and fore-finger, lets them go, and they make a loud, wet, smacking sound. So that all I can think about is fish slapping against the water. "So I was just reading a little bit about Pelé."

"Who?"

"Pelé. You know, the world famous soccer player?"

"Never heard of him."

"Oh? Really?" He looks at his fingernails and then mumbles to himself, "That's the trouble with kids. Never read. So what can you expect?"

"You talking to me?" I ask.

"No, my mistake," he mumbles, as he picks up a folder with my name on the side of it and puts on a pair of half-glasses. "My mistake. He only revolutionized the game of soccer. My mistake." He clears his throat. Looks up at me and gives me a big smile. "Now suppose we get down to business?" He clears his throat again. "So, Mac, tell me. It seems that you've got something on your mind. Do you want to talk about it?"

"No."

"Why not?"

"Nothing to talk about."

"Yes, of course." He closes his eyes and smiles like he's just heard something that makes him real happy. "I've heard that many times. And, in fact, Mac, you may not believe this, but I have said those very words myself many times when I've been upset. There's nothing to talk about. That is a very common response to what you might feel is someone probing into your affairs. But I should hasten to add that only when one talks about things that are bothering him does one free oneself from those things." He folds his arms over his stomach, smiles, and then pinches his lips between his thumb and forefinger. "Well?"

"Well?"

"What do you have to say?"

"Nothing."

"I see." He nods knowingly. "Do you want to tell me why you punched Shawn?"

"No."

"You don't feel like talking about it."

"Not really."

"Do you want to tell me why you don't want to talk about it?"

"No."

"You're feeling pretty negative, aren't you?"

"What's that mean?"

"It means everything I say, you negate."

"I don't know what that means."

"It means you don't want to talk about anything."

"That's right."

"Why?"

"Because this place sucks."

"That's no reason not to talk. I talk plenty when I'm in a place that I don't like, or if I feel happy, or if I feel sad. So tell me how you felt when you punched Shawn."

"Why?"

"It'll help us understand what's going on inside that noggin of yours. Now just close your eyes and think about how you felt."

I just sit there. And stare at the floor. And try to space out.

"What do you remember?" I hear Cartledge's voice off in the distance.

"Nothing."

"You're hiding something from me, Mac."

"No, I'm not."

"Yes, you are."

"No, I'm not."

"Mac." He blows out air so that his lips flap. "I'm feeling a lot of negativity from you right now."

Suddenly I have a headache. My throat aches. I feel like I'm about to gag.

"I think I'm going to throw up."

"Don't be rude, young man."

"I mean it." I stand up.

"Sit down, I tell you."

"I'm going to throw up."

"No, you're not. You're going to sit down."

"I have to go to the bathroom."

"You are not excused from this counseling session."

I throw up all over his gray leather boots.

"Oh, disgusting!" He coughs into his hands. "This is disgusting. Get out of my office at once. Get out. This minute."

25

Haven't seen Jenny for weeks. Except in the halls. I try to carry my books with me all the time now so I don't have to use my locker. And run into her by accident. It's better that way. Except this morning. This morning I'm standing in front of my locker — staring at it like it's a video game or something — when she interrupts.

"Hello." God, how her voice gives me the chills.

"Hi," I say, to the top shelf in my locker.

"Are you going to have breakfast?" she asks.

I look at my watch. There's twenty minutes to homeroom. I'm too stupid to think of an excuse. "Yes."

"Can I sit with you?" I nod without looking at her. Kick the door of my locker closed. Turn and stare at her. Embarrassed. It's been weeks since we've been this close. And for some reason this morning I notice her eyes. They're blue. Like the flame on the tip of a Bunsen burner.

The cafeteria is nearly empty. We pick up trays and slide them along the stainless steel counter. Glasses of orange juice stand in orange puddles. Jenny passes them by. I take one. And a plate of scrambled eggs. She stops at the hot water and coffee canisters. Pours herself a cup of steaming water. Takes a tea bag. I turn the black handle of the coffee canister and watch bubbles rise in the glass stem. Hot coffee spills into a cracked cup. I put the cup on a red-rimmed saucer. And follow Jenny to the cashier.

We sit at a table away from the windows. Next to a clanking radiator. She sips her tea. I eat the cold eggs I didn't even want and sip the sour coffee. What are we going to talk about? What am I going to say? Jenny, there's something wrong. Can't you see? There's something wrong with me. I finish the eggs. Drink the orange juice. Look across the table. Jenny's looking at me with those blue eyes of hers.

"So . . . have you been skiing much?" she asks.

"No." I trace the crack on the coffee cup with my thumb.

"I can't believe it. How come?"

"I just don't feel like it." I look at her from behind the cup. It's warm in my hands. "I've been thinking about other stuff . . . like running away." She turns her head from me like I slapped her or something. I should shut up but I don't. "You ever think about running away?"

"No." She picks up a napkin and wipes her hands like she's not going to say anything. But then she does. "Maybe when I was a little kid . . . maybe when Mom and Dad were splitting up. Are you really thinking about running away? Because I was thinking of asking you if you wanted to see Dire Straits with me, but if you're not going to be around . . ."

I put the cup down in the saucer. It's grown cold in my hands. And stare across the cafeteria. At the green cinder block wall. In the middle there's this clock. Hanging there as lonely as Jesus. Its arms say only five minutes until homeroom.

"What did you say?" I ask, still looking at the clock.

"Are you really thinking about running away?"

"I mean about Dire Straits?"

79

"I asked if you wanted to see them in concert."

"When?"

"Next month."

"If I'm still around."

"You're serious about this, aren't you?"

"Sort of."

"Why?"

"Because I've got my parents coming in to talk to me and Rosen. That's why."

"How come?"

"How come?" I push my chair back from the table. Stand up and grab my tray. She stands up and puts her half-filled cup of tea on my empty plate of scrambled eggs. "Because I've been screwing up."

"How come?" She follows me to the drop-off cart. I dump the tray on the cart. And push through the brown swinging doors into the main hall. It's like suddenly walking into a traffic jam or something. Kids everywhere. I stop and wait for an opening. Jenny waits with me. I turn and look at her real quick.

"I don't know," I finally answer.

She doesn't say anything. Just looks at me. Her blue eyes burning holes right through me.

• 26 •

"Well?" says Mr. Rosen. He's sitting on the edge of his desk.

"Answer Mr. Rosen." My mother sits on the edge of the couch and stares at me. I stare back at her. She's smiling.

But underneath the smile I can tell her face is angry and tight. Dad is sitting next to her. He's smiling too. Like a jerk. With the school cat sitting on his lap.

"Go ahead and answer him, Mac."

I look at Mr. Rosen. He's smiling, too. I think maybe I missed a joke. What was the joke? Can anybody please tell me what the joke is?

"What's so funny?" I ask.

"Nothing's funny." Dad smiles at me.

"This is all very serious," Mr. Rosen adds. I guess I didn't miss anything. "Now, how about answering my question?"

"How can I answer your question if I don't know what it is?" Mr. Rosen rubs his hands together slowly. I can hear his dry skin crackling. He speaks slowly but steadily. Like a dump truck backing up.

"I guess you didn't hear me, Mac." He puts his hands down beside his legs and gently lifts himself just off the desk. I watch him, amazed at how he hangs in midair. Then, very slowly, he lets himself down. The whole time he doesn't once take his eyes off of me.

"There are a number of things your parents and I are concerned about, Mac. And we want to take them up with you one at a time."

Good for you. Take them any way you want.

"A lot of what we're seeing from you is uncharacteristic of . . . Mac?"

I'm looking around the room. I want to find a crack in the wall to crawl into. "What?"

He pushes himself off the desk and walks towards me.

"You just haven't been yourself lately, Mac. From punching Shawn in the mouth, to failing grades, to being rude to Mr. Cartledge."

"I wasn't rude to him. He was rude to me."

"That's enough of that, Mac. You asked to hear my question. So let me finish. I'm trying to be as clear as I can. All right?" He's standing so close to me his knees are almost touching my knees. I can smell his sweat mixed with cologne. I can see the skin under his beard. A gold watch chain is looped around his neck. It disappears into his vest pocket. I'd like to yank that chain right off his neck. But I don't. I just sit there. And look away.

"As I said, Mac, we're very concerned about this behavior because it's not like you. Your parents and I talked on the phone and, after comparing notes, decided on this meeting. They tell me that you've given up skiing. Is that right?"

"I just haven't started yet." I look down at the rug. A yellow piece of thread is unraveling at the edge. I cover it with my foot.

"Good. Good. That's good. I'm glad. Because you know how much we need you on our ski team."

"Sure," I mumble to myself. "I know."

He turns and nods his head at my parents. Like it's such a big deal. Then he walks back across the room to his desk. "So, after comparing notes with your parents, we decided we should get together and have this little talk. We also think that you should continue to talk with Mr. Cartledge. That was my question, Mac. Will you meet with him, say once every week or so, just to —"

"No," I interrupt.

"Mac." My father pushes the cat off his lap and leans towards me. "Think before you answer! Please."

My mother's face is white. She looks down at the watch on her wrist. The cat rubs its back against her brown stockings. She shoves it away with the tip of her shoe. Mr. Rosen picks it up. He hooks it under his arm so that it stares across the room at me with its ugly, wet eyes.

"Why not, Mac?"

"I talked to him already."

"And?" He stares at me just like the cat.

"I already told you. Cartledge is a jerk."

"Mac." My mother squeezes her wrist so tight her hand turns red.

"I take it you don't like him." Mr. Rosen puts the cat down on his desk. He clasps his hands together and spins on his heel until he's facing my parents.

"Well," my father says in his most serious voice, "maybe there is somebody else."

"Precisely my thought. Suppose," Mr. Rosen begins, "suppose that you talked to somebody besides Mr. Cartledge." He stops and looks at me as if I'm supposed to answer him. I don't answer so he keeps talking.

"Suppose you talked with another counselor instead of Mr. Cartledge. Would you agree to do that?"

"Do I have a choice?"

"Actually, Mac, you probably don't have a choice."

"So why'd you ask?"

"Well, because you can either meet with another counselor, or —"

"Or what?"

"Mac." My mother looks at me. And I see a sadness under her tight face I've never seen before. Like any minute she's going to cry. I look down at the rug. When I look back at her I see tears in her eyes. I don't know how long they've been there.

"Or you can meet with me every day," Mr. Rosen finishes.

I don't answer. I can't do anything but look away from my mother's face.

"Well, Mac, what'll it be?" Mr. Rosen is leaning against my chair, rocking it with his knee.

"I don't know."

"Sound okay to you?"

"I guess."

"Good. You'll begin tomorrow."

"With who?"

"With whom." He kicks the chair with his foot.

"With whom," I mumble.

"Oh, I'll find someone. Don't worry about that." He hits me lightly on the shoulder. "I'll find someone who'll knock some sense into you." He looks at my parents. "So, we'll begin tomorrow."

"Tomorrow? Tomorrow I won't be here. Tomorrow I'm gonna be sick."

"Like hell you are." Mr. Rosen doesn't even look at me. He picks up a folder on his desk. "You'll be here."

"Yeah?"

He looks up from the folder. "Yeah. Even if I have to drag you in here by your hair."

84

I hardly say a word on the way home. I sit in the back and stare out the window. There isn't much to see. It's dark. My parents keep saying dumb things to me.

"What do you think, Mac?"

"That Mr. Rosen sure is some guy."

"We're on the right track now, Mac. Don't you think?"

"He'll come up with a hell of a counselor, Mac. I just know he will."

"Mac?" My mother leans back between the bucket seats. Rests her hands on the long black handle of the emergency break. "Say something, honey."

"What do you want me to say?"

"What you're thinking."

"You don't want to hear that." I turn away from the window and look at her face in the dark. I can see the outline of her small nose and chin against the windshield. Then the car goes into a curve and she swings out of sight. I look back out the window.

"Mac." She leans back between the seats. "I want to hear what you're thinking."

"No, you don't."

"Yes, I do." She swings back out of sight. "Dan, will you not drive so fast, please!"

"Sorry." My father lets up on the gas.

"I'm trying to talk with Mac. Now, Mac." My mother swings back into sight. "I think you have to admit that Mr. Rosen really cares."

"About what?" I look up at her but she's gone again.

"Dan." My mother's getting hyper. "I asked you to slow down."

"I already slowed down. What do you want us to do? Crawl home?"

"How about driving the speed limit?"

"I'm going thirty miles an hour."

"Then go twenty-five. I'm trying to talk to our son." She swings back into sight. "Now, Mac, I want to ask you something. Are you listening?"

Yes, dammit. "I'm listening."

"Should we get a dog?"

What is she talking about now? "A dog?"

"Yes, a dog." She starts to swing out of sight again. But grabs the back of the driver's seat. "The twins would love a dog."

Terrific, the twins want a dog.

"It would be so good for them and us and you."

And make everything better, right? "I don't want a dog."

"Mac . . ."

"Tonight in Washington," the radio blares through the back speakers, "the president will give . . ."

"Dan." My mother swings out of sight. Furious. "I am talking." She reaches for the radio to turn it off but grabs the volume control instead and spins it the wrong way. The noise from the speakers nearly lifts the roof off the car. And I can almost feel a wind whipping through my hair. My father switches off the radio.

"Daniel!" my mother shouts. "What is going on?"

"Just a news conference, dear." And he steps on the gas.

"Daniel!" She leans back in her seat. And I can't tell if she's laughing or crying. Then she calls back to me, "We'll talk later."

Terrific. I lean against the window. My teeth vibrating against the glass. The window colder than Novocain against my lips.

• 28 •

Everyone's talking at once. Except me. I don't say a word. I don't eat a thing. I just sit there at the table and try not to stare at the ketchup-covered bones on my plate. I look down at my right hand lying next to the blue dinner plate. I'm rolling a fork between my fingers. The fork makes a pattern of shadow and light as I roll it. It's not much, but it's enough to keep my eyes off the bones. Otherwise I'd throw up.

"Mac." I hear a voice calling my name. I concentrate as hard as I can not to hear it. "Mac." The voice grows louder. I recognize that voice. I've known it my whole life. I try closing my ears by squinting hard. It helps some. "Mac." But it's not totally effective. So I close my eyes. That helps. It blocks everything out. Until I feel a hand shaking my shoulder. I look at the hand. The skin is white and wrinkled. I know that hand. The fingernails are torn and uneven. The knuckles are round and white. The fingers are long and fat. I know those fingers.

"Mac." Yes, I know that voice. I look up into the brown eyes. At the high cheekbones. The crooked teeth. The big

87

smile. The brown and gray hair whisking back over the big ears. I know that face.

"Mac, are you all right?" I know those words. I know what they mean. "Mac, are you all right?"

"Get your hands off of me," I shout into that face. *"Get your filthy hands off of me."* I feel the hand move away. Then I feel it pinching my arm. Like vise grips. *"I said, take your hands off of me,"* I shout again. Those eyes are squinting. The cheeks are red and pinched together. The lips are tight around crooked teeth. The ceiling rushes towards me. Suddenly I feel like I'm standing. The fork drops from my hand. I hear it hit the plate. Then it's like I'm flying out of the room. My head is hanging over one of my shoulders like it can't catch up to me. I see the dinner table floating off to my left. And the faces of my stupid brothers hanging over their plates of ketchup-covered bones. Their mouths open. Like they've never seen a kid flying out of the dining room before. But I know what's going on. I know who's behind all this. I'm no asshole.

"I said, take your fucking hands off of me."

"Watch the chair," the voice mutters into my ear. I watch for the chair and we veer off through the living room. Out into the hall. And up the front stairs. My arms and shoulder are numb. It feels like all I have on that side of my body is the imprint of a hand. I try and count the dowels in the white banister. But they fly by too fast.

"Up," the voice whispers. My legs do as they're told like they belong to the voice. They fly up the steps. Down the hall. Into the family room. Until my nose is rubbing against a rung of the ladder to my room. I'm not out of breath but I stand there panting. Then the voice.

"Up," it whispers. I start up the ladder. The hand still on my arm. We rise slowly towards the door to my room. I feel the rungs in my hands. And on the soles of my feet. Then I'm standing over my bed. Looking down at the gray blankets. A hand reaches down and pulls the gray blankets back. And I'm looking at white sheets.

"Lie down." The voice in my ear. I put my hands out in front of me and slide down onto the sheets. I feel the blankets settling over me. I hear a click. The lights go off. Night rushes into the room. I can feel it moving over my neck.

"Good night, Mac," the voice calls from the ladder.

"Good night, Dad," I call back. And suddenly my arm starts aching and I begin to cry. I jam my head under the pillow to stop the tears. But they follow me like darkness.

• 29 •

I wake up to the sound of someone screaming. I look up. Nothing but night all around me. I reach over and turn on the bedside lamp. The light explodes across the room. I cover my eyes with my hands. I can hear myself breathing. Like I just ran a mile. I swallow slowly. My throat is tight and sore. I squint through my fingers at the clock. Slowly the numbers come into focus. It's two forty-five. I lean back against my pillow and listen. I can't hear anything but my own breathing. And I'm cold and wet. I lift up the blankets and my shirt is soaked with sweat. I kick off the covers and stand next to the bed, shivering. Pull off the wet shirt and pants. Put on a sweat suit. Crawl back into bed and pull the covers up over my head.

"Mac?" a voice calls from downstairs, sending shivers down my spine. "Are you all right?"

"Yes." I pull the blankets tighter around my shoulders.

"You had a bad dream?"

"No."

"Well, you sure screamed loud enough."

"Screamed?" It was me who screamed?

"Why don't you turn your light off?" He climbs up the ladder so his head is sticking through the doorway. "Are you sure you're okay?"

"Yeah." I click off my light.

"Good. Now no more screaming." His voice backs down the ladder.

"Yeah." I roll over on my side. "No more screaming."

I lie there, staring into the dark. Trying not to shiver. Trying to stay on the dry part of the sheet. Trying not to remember the sound of the scream that woke me up. Trying not to remember the dream. I close my eyes and try to sleep. But I can't. Someone's hairy legs are standing over me. I sit up sweaty and shivering. Quickly turn on the lights. The legs disappear. I swallow. My throat is sore. My head aches. I pull the blankets up around me. What should I do? I try and think. What should I do? I shove a tape into the stereo and pull on the earphones. Music roars through my head like water. Only three hours until morning. I can wait it out. Even though I have nothing to wait for. Nothing. Nothing but school. Nothing but listening to another dumb-ass counselor tell me what to do.

I wake up to the alarm blaring in the distance. The earphones are pressed tight to my ears. The tape deck clicking like a heart trying to stop beating. Never have I been so glad to hear that alarm. I slap the top of it. Pull off the earphones. And climb out of bed. In the shower I stand so the spray burns a hole in my head. The water spilling over my eyes like bandages. And later at breakfast I sit there. Not saying a word, staring at my eggs.

"Are you going to eat anything?" My father is standing behind me. I shrug. "You really should eat something, Mac. Especially after the night you had." He takes the plate from me. "I'll heat them up."

"I don't want them heated up," I say through closed teeth.

"How else are you going to eat them?"

"I'm not."

"Yes, you are."

"Okay. I am. Go ahead. Run my life. See if I care. You think I care?" I look up at him. His face is dotted with little black beard hairs. You think I care? I grab the plate from him. What do I care? What do I care about anything? I grab a handful of scrambled eggs and stuff it into my mouth.

"There," I gag. "How's that?"

• 30 •

I'm sitting in civics. My book is propped up on the desk in front of me blocking the sun that's pouring in through the high windows. Mrs. Miller is talking about town meetings

91

and moderators, I think, but I don't know. Because I'm looking at the world map on the wall. The sun spilling across it like meteorites. And I'm wondering why Russia is yellow. Why China is gray. Why England and Poland and India are pink. When somebody calls my name. I look up.

"Mac." It's Mrs. Miller. She's holding a note in her hand and there's a kid with a brown sweater standing next to her. She catches my eye over the top of the book. "You're wanted downstairs."

"Oooh," someone whispers behind me. I turn to stare at the voice. It's Woody. "Big trouble now," he whispers through closed lips.

"Shut up, Woody," I say out loud. I close the civics book. Slide it into my book bag and stand up.

"So tough," he whispers back.

"Have fun." Brook smiles stupidly.

"That's enough talking, boys." Mrs. Miller is resting her wrists on her hips. "Simply because Mac is leaving gives you no right to talk without permission."

"It's a free world," Woody whispers.

"Yeah, it's a democracy," Shawn echoes.

"What did you say, boys?"

"We said, we want to hear more about the democracy of town meetings," Woody answers quickly.

"Good. But just one minute. Mac?" Mrs. Miller steps to her desk. I stop where I am. In front of the world map. I look over at her through the sunspots. I can see bits of her hair and part of her neck.

"Pages one thirty-three to one thirty-seven for tonight, Mac." Her voice burns through the sunspots.

"Yes."

"Well, write down your homework."

"Yes." I pull my assignment book out of my bag and scribble, HOMEWORK.

"Got it?" Her voice shoots across the room. I squint through the sun. Her hair and face go in and out of focus.

"Got it."

"Good. Oh, while you're there, Mac, please roll up that map."

"This one?" I reach out and touch the map's smooth oilskin.

"Please." Her voice rockets back through the sunspots. I turn and reach down for the little metal handle. My shadow falls across the map. So that most of the world's in darkness. The only color I can see is the blue of the North Pole. I yank down the ring and the map snaps closed. My shadow disappears into the blackboard.

"Thank you. Better get going now."

"Yes." I slide down the aisle and out the door as quickly as I can.

The hallway is as dark as a cave. I stand outside the closed door and listen. To dead silence. Except for the muffled voice of Mrs. Miller. The student who came for me is gone. I start slowly down the hall towards the stairs. Past the janitor's office and the Coke machine. The metal treads on the stairs seem unusually worn. I run my hand on the wooden banister. Instead of being smooth, it's sticky to the touch. I rest on the landing. I'm in no hurry. Not to go sit with some jerk like Cartledge.

At the top of the stairs I look down the hall. It's as long

93

and empty as a runway. I start down it. Barely moving. Halfway there I pass the front door. I stop and look out. Water is running across the sidewalk. Snow must be melting. I turn and walk out through the double doors. The bright sun slaps me in the face. I don't know where I'm going. I step across the wet sidewalk and out into the parking lot. I step around the large puddles and walk through the small ones. Surrounded by cars. All different colors. Like the world map. Which one is China? I spot a gray car one row over. I always wanted to visit China. I walk over to it. Try the door. It opens. I climb in and sit on the red driver's seat. It's warm to the touch. Even through my long underwear. For a minute I stare at the green dials and gauges. Then I look through the windshield up towards the mountain. I can just make out the cables of a chair lift through the tops of the trees. I smile to myself. Thinking about what I'm missing. Nobody will find me here. I lean back into the seat and close my eyes.

I never hear the door open. I just feel the cold air. When I turn, I see part of a three-piece suit. The part with the vest. All the buttons are buttoned. The head and legs are missing.

"Must have made a wrong turn somewhere, Mac." He steps back. I see his knees and neck.

"You're late," I hear myself say as I climb out of the car.

He slips a gold watch out of his vest pocket. Snaps open the gold cover like a butterfly wing. And looks at it casually. "So I am." He snaps it shut. "Next time I'll send an armed guard for you." He coughs lightly into his free hand. "Now, may I escort you to your new counselor, sir?"

I don't say anything. Just follow him through the parking lot back into the school. He stops outside the door to the counselor's office. I stand in the middle of the hallway. He motions me closer. I take half a step towards him. He puts a hand to his mouth and says in a low voice, "The name of your new counselor is Mrs. Resnick."

"Mrs. Resnick. That's a woman."

"Very good, Mac. I think we're on the right track."

"But I don't want to see a woman."

"Listen, Mac." I hate it when Mr. Rosen says, Listen, Mac, like that. "You didn't want to talk to a man either. Who do you want to talk to?"

"Nobody."

"Sorry, Mac. That's not in the cards. But I'll tell you what. Give Mrs. Resnick a shot. If you don't like her, I'm sure I can do something with my schedule so that you and I can meet every day." I don't answer. I just stare at the door of the counselor's office. Trying to look through it.

"Well, what do you say?"

I shrug my shoulders.

"Good." I feel his hand slapping me on the back. "Now, no games with her, Mac. You understand?"

"I'm not playing games."

• 31 •

I step into the room. The door closes behind me. I look at the bookshelf where Cartledge would be standing. No one's there. I look over towards the window. Where his files would be. There are no files. But there's a couch under the window. And sitting at one end of the couch is a lady. With more red hair than I've ever seen in my whole life. Her face is pale white. Except for the freckles that I can see clear across the room. Her hands are folded in her lap. She's wearing a dress the color of the couch, so she kind of blends in to it. It's almost as if she's not there.

"Well, Mac, I'm glad you made it. Come sit down."

I walk slowly across the room and sit down on a folding chair.

"I'm Mrs. Resnick."

"I know."

"Yes. Well, I just wanted to tell you myself." She stops and looks at me closely. "It's kind of an unusual name, isn't it?"

"No," I lie.

"Well, there's only one in the phone book. Anyway . . . to change the subject. I'm kind of in a jam. And I sort of need your help."

"My help?" I look at her like she just asked me a trick question.

"Yeah, it's a royal mess. They think they need these records at the superintendent's office right now." She holds up a folder. "But I'm supposed to be seeing you. So I was hoping you wouldn't mind driving along with me — maybe we could talk some in the car. What do you think?"

"Sure." I'd rather ride in a car than talk in some dumb office any day.

"Good." She reaches down on the couch and picks up a quilted winter coat. I follow her out into the faculty park-

96

ing lot. She climbs into a red Chevette and I get in the passenger side.

The next thing I know we're cruising down Route 9. And she's talking the whole time. About all the stupid paperwork they make her do in the school system. I don't say a word. I just half listen to her and half watch the river winding along beside us. Then she starts asking me stuff about skiing and soccer. And we talk the whole way there. Even when she's parking the car in front of some big brick building. She's asking about ski waxes.

"This will only take a second," she says, getting out of the car and slamming the door. I watch her run up the front steps of the building and pull open a gray door. Two minutes later she comes running back down the steps. Her red hair is flying through the air. She jumps in the car and we're off again. This time headed back to school.

"Are you hungry?" She looks at me as we pull out on Route 9. I shrug. "Well, I am dying of hunger, and I just remembered that I forgot to have breakfast. Do you mind if we stop for something?"

"No." Why should I mind? Watching her eat something is a hundred times better than sitting in civics.

Two miles later she pulls up at the Curbside diner and parks next to a red pickup. I follow her into the restaurant. She chooses a booth by the window. I sit across from her. She picks up the menu and studies it. I study the cracks on the yellow tabletop.

"How about some pancakes?" She looks at me from over the top of the menu. "With real syrup?" She opens her eyes wide. They're green.

97

"Can I help you?" A tall woman with big red hands stands at the end of the table. She's holding a tiny pad in one hand and a pencil in the other.

"You sure can. We'll have two orders of pancakes. A cup of coffee for me and what do you want, Mac?"

"Coffee, I guess."

"You'll like these pancakes." Mrs. Resnick looks me right in the eye. "You'll really like them a lot."

The tall lady slides two cups of coffee and a small pitcher of cream onto the table.

"Just what I needed." She smiles at me over her steaming cup of coffee. I bend down to my cup and sip it lightly. "Now just wait until you try these pancakes."

Five minutes later the lady with the big red hands drops two plates covered with pancakes onto our table. She leans back towards the counter and grabs two little tin pitchers.

"Here. One hundred percent maple syrup," she says with a huge smile. "Enjoy."

"We will." Mrs. Resnick smiles back.

I don't say anything. I just stare at the pancakes, light brown and huge. Steam spiraling into the air. Big scoops of butter melting, spilling off the pancakes onto the plate. It's enough to make the back of my mouth ache. I look up at Mrs. Resnick. She's pouring the maple syrup over her pancakes.

"Doesn't that just look terrific?" She looks up at me. I pick up the tin of syrup and pour it across my own pancakes. Then I pick up a fork and start eating. I dip a piece of pancake in a puddle of melted butter and syrup. It's almost too big for my mouth. But I chew around it and don't look up from my plate until I'm done. When I finish she asks me if I've had enough. I nod. She walks over to the cash register, and the lady with the red hands rings up the bill. Then we go out to the car. The sun's gone under. But it's still warm.

"What a day." She spreads her arms out wide, the sleeves of her winter coat like wings. "Listen to that river, Mac. Just listen." Water and ice are roaring downstream. So loud I can't hear the cars and trucks whirring past on Route 9.

• 32 •

She parks behind the school. Turns off the engine and looks at me. Now it's going to come, I think. Now I'm going to get counseled. Now I'm going to get fixed.

"Well, Mac, time to get back to work."

"Right." They all think I'm so dumb. Like I don't know what's going on. I sit there and wait for her lecture. Always a thousand lectures.

"Thanks for having breakfast with me." She opens the door and steps out of the car. When I look up from the floor all I see is the door closing behind her. By the time I get out of the car she's halfway up the walk to the school. I have to run to catch her. She pushes open the side door. Steps inside. And leans against it to let me in. I follow her into the counselors' waiting room. Where the secretary sits and kids wait to see counselors. The secretary's on the phone. But when she sees Mrs. Resnick she waves a handful of pink slips at her. She takes them and steps into her office. I follow her. She closes the door behind us.

"Will you look at this?" She waves the slips of paper at me like they're homework or something. Then she picks up the phone. "Your books are right there." She points to the chair as she dials with the black receiver in her hand. "And thanks for having breakfast with me. I really enjoyed it."

"Is . . . that . . . ah, it?" I ask, as I reach down and pick up my book bag.

"I'm afraid so." She puts the phone to her ear.

"But I thought, you know, I was supposed to . . . I mean, Mr. Rosen said I should, you know, that we should . . ."

"Yes, Mac?"

I look up from the floor. "I thought that —"

"Hello. Yes. Hello, Dr. Kline? Yes. This is Elizabeth Resnick. I'm fine. And how are you?" She waves her hand at me. "That's nice. Can you hold the line for just one second? Thank you." She puts the receiver against her waist.

"I'm sorry, Mac. You had a question."

I shrug my shoulders. "Mr. Rosen said I was supposed to, you know, talk and stuff . . . once a week."

"I see." She puts her free hand to her chin, curling her fingers around her jaw like she's thinking.

"So, ah, are we gonna . . . I mean, you know, meet again?"

"That would be nice. I'd really enjoy that." She looks right at me. Her green eyes like a light I have to look into.

I wait for her to say something. "Why don't you make an appointment with Marge? And I'll see you then. Okay? Now, you'll have to excuse me. I have a ton of calls to make."

She takes the phone off her waist and puts it to her ear. "Hello, Dr. Kline? I'm sorry. I just had to answer a quick question for a friend of mine."

· 33 ·

Marge is on the phone too. I stand there and stare at the wire baskets on her desk. One says IN. The other says OUT.

There are two kids sitting against the wall. One's a big kid. Maybe six feet, two hundred pounds. Never seen him before. He must be new. Poor kid. He's got more pimples on his face than the Rocky Mountains got peaks, as Woody would say. The other kid is a girl reading a book. She's got brown hair. And three different kinds of earrings dangling from each ear.

"Can I help you?" Marge looks at me through a pair of glasses as big as ski goggles.

"I'm supposed to make an appointment to see Mrs. Resnick."

"Very good. Now, when did she want to see you?"

"She said that was between the two of us."

"Oh, she did, did she?" She picks up a black date book and begins to finger through the pages. "Let me see. How about March twentieth?"

"That's a month from now."

101

"So it is." She thumbs back through the book.

"Well, in that case." She keeps thumbing. "How about a week from today? At two-thirty?"

"Okay." I take a pen out of a black cup on her desk and write the time on the back of my English notebook. I start to leave when the phone rings. She answers it. Nods her head and hangs up.

"Bill," she calls across the room to the big kid, "Mrs. Resnick will see you now." I watch him stand up. He's even bigger than I thought. He walks across the room and into her office without even knocking.

I lean against Marge's desk. "Who's that?"

"That's Bill." She swivels her chair around so that she's facing her typewriter.

"What's he doing in there?"

"I imagine he's talking with the counselor." She rolls a piece of paper into the typewriter. "Just like you."

"What do you mean, just like me?"

"I mean, they're talking just like you were. But they're probably talking about different things. I would imagine. Wouldn't you?"

"Yeah," I mutter, as I start backing out the door. "But I wouldn't count on it." We didn't talk about anything.

"Hey, kid, watch where you're going!" a voice growls behind me. But too late. I back right into somebody who's as soft as a pillow except for the elbows. I turn to see who it is. It's Cartledge standing in the doorway. When he sees me he quickly steps backwards into the hall. His gray leather boots make a soft scuffling sound on the linoleum.

"So." He puts his hand to his head. Patting the strands of hair over his baldness. "Mac." He nearly shouts my name. "Feeling better?"

"No," I whisper. And walk right past him. Slowly. As I do he back-pedals quickly across the hall. Right into three girls.

"Excuse me." He jumps out of their way. "I'm so sorry."

"Oh, that's okay, Mr. Cartledge," the smallest girl giggles. "You couldn't see us."

I keep walking down the hall. And when I get to the stairs I can still hear him. Flirting his fool head off.

• 34 •

It's Friday night. End of the week. And I'm stuck with the little creeps again. I don't cook them the usual supper. Just slit open a loaf of white bread. Spin open jars of peanut butter and strawberry jam. And the two of them stand at the counter. Knives in their fists. Spreading peanut butter and jam across the bread. I don't go near them. But lie on the living room floor next to the wood-burning stove.

"Mac, milk!" Peter shouts at me after ten minutes.

"Peter, icebox!" I shout back.

"Mac, napkins!" Avery stands in the doorway holding his hands in the air. Peanut butter and jam dripping from his face to his fingers.

"Don't come near me," I shout.

"Mac, napkins," he moans.

"Okay." I get up. "Okay." Grab him by his turtleneck and pull him over to the sink.

"What are you doing?" he asks.

I don't say anything but grab the sprayer. Spin on the tap. And hose him down. Forehead to fingernails.

"Mac, you're drowning me," he cries.

But I don't stop until I see the white of his skin.

"Mac, I got peanut butter in my eyes," he cries again.

I hand him a paper towel. He dries his face. Snarling at me. When he looks up I stare at him. Like he's lucky to be alive. He gets the message. And disappears upstairs, yelling over his shoulder. Peter hasn't moved. He's still leaning over the counter. Stuffing his face. I stand there staring at him until he looks over at me. A big smile on his face.

"What's so funny, fatso?"

"Avery," he giggles, "got peanut butter in his eyes."

"Yeah? You're not much better." And I grab him by the collar and haul him upstairs.

"I ain't fat," he mutters up the steps. "I'm just big for my age."

"Yeah?" I pull him into the bathroom. In front of the mirror. "You're pretty filthy for your age, too."

He looks at me in the mirror. I look at him. He looks at himself. And laughs.

"You're a mess," I shout.

"You don't have to yell. Avery, come look at me," he shouts. And out of nowhere Avery peers into the mirror from behind my back. Their eyes connect in the glass and they both laugh like retards. I grab them by their collars and shake them until they stop laughing.

"Cut it out, Mac. That hurts." Peter twists away from me.

"In the bath, you guys," I shout.

"No bath." Avery looks up at me. "I just had a shower."

I don't say anything but open the taps. Water spits out of the spout. And rushes into the tub.

"We don't want no bath," Peter snarls at me over the noise of rushing water.

"Yeah?" I snarl right back. They both look at me. Then at the tub. "Get your filthy bodies clean."

"Which boat you want, Petey?" Avery begins to undress.

"The sub." Peter pulls his shirt over his head. "The one with the humongous torpedoes."

• 35 •

I don't want to be near them while they're in the bath. So I go downstairs and stare at the mess they've made. The peanut butter jar is empty except for peanut butter dripping down its side. The jar of jam's scraped clean. The jug of milk is open, smeared with peanut butter. The countertop looks like the inside of a sandwich.

"Who the hell's going to clean this up?" I mutter at the mess. Then I get an idea. I grab a couple of pieces of bread and, using them like a sponge, wipe the counter clean. I get out two clean plates. Drop the bread smeared with peanut butter and jam on them and carry them upstairs to the twins' room. I put a plate on each pillow. Then I lie down on the floor, kind of pleased with myself, and wait for them.

I stare at the ceiling, at all their Lego spaceships hanging on fishing line. Like they're cruising through space. In the middle of them all, and turning slowly in the air, is Peter's death star. A few inches above it is an empty spider's web. Its own galaxy. I wonder what it would be like in outer space, away from everything. And everybody. And all the dumb things they make you do.

"What's that?" Peter's the first out of the bath. His cheeks are red. His hair's wet.

"What?"

"This." He picks up the glass plate from his pillow.

"Snack," I mumble.

"Snack?" He holds up the mangled bread. "Hey, Ave, Mac made us a snack." He takes a bite of the bread. "Peanut butter and jam. Thanks, Mac."

"Don't mention it." And the two of them stand next to their beds. Towels drooping under their arms. Smacking down the peanut butter. I roll over and lean up on an elbow.

"Suckers." I try to laugh but can't. "Joke's on you. You know what you just ate?"

"Nope."

I tell them.

"So?" They could care less.

"So where are my pajamas?" Peter looks around the room.

"So I could have given you guys a sponge and you would have eaten it."

"Here they are, Petey." Avery lifts up the corner of the green rug and pulls out a pair of pajamas.

"Stupid me." Peter slaps his head with the fat of his hand.

"I said, I could have given you guys poison for a snack and you would have eaten it."

"Sure, Mac." Peter pulls on his pajamas in slow motion. I get tired of holding my head in the air. I let it drop onto my arms. And doze off. When I wake up the light's different. Brighter and darker. A night wind is blowing through the room. The curtains are still. Peter and Avery are in the next room. Whispering sounds of spaceships and rockets.

"Fly your guy over here, Petey, okay?"

"Okay." Sounds of lasers and torn engines crash through the air. "Shit. He's hit, Ave."

"He's falling."

"Sonofabitch."

"Sonofabitch." And silence. Not even the sound of a crash. Or the night wind. Just silence. Until I think I'm asleep again.

"Petey?" Avery's whisper wakes me.

"What?"

"Is God real?"

"What?"

"Is God real?"

"Do you think he's real?"

"I asked you first."

"I don't know." He makes the sound of a computer processing bits of information. "Maybe he's like Santa Claus."

"What do you mean, like Santa Claus?"

"He was real once. But now he's not."

"Yeah, Petey, but I know Santa's real. Because he brings presents."

"So?"

"So God doesn't bring presents."

"So God isn't real," I mumble. But they don't hear me. Because the phone's ringing.

"I got it," Peter screams.

"I got it," Avery screams right behind him.

It stops ringing.

"I got it."

"I got it."

"Say hello," I shout.

"It's for you," Avery shouts back.

For me. Terrific. Just what I need. A phone call. I get up. And the side of my head smashes into the death star. A direct hit. I back away. Dazed from the contact.

"Hey, Mac," Avery scolds me as he runs back into the room. "I thought Petey said to leave his death star alone."

· 36 ·

The door closes behind me. I stand there. My back sweaty. My knees like they're going to buckle. Blood pumping through my hands. I look over to the couch. She's not there. I turn and expect to see her at her desk. On the phone. But she's not there either. The office is empty. I'm no asshole. I know what's going on. I start to leave.

The hall door opens and she backs into the room talking too loud. I stand there swaying back and forth. Not sure if I'm going or staying. Looking at her. The same red hair. All over the place. The same crazy-colored clothes. She closes the door. Turns and looks at me.

"Mac!" She throws her hands up in the air like I'm a surprise or something. "Let's blow this joint."

"What?"

"Let's blow this joint." She says it in a weird accent.

"What do you mean?"

"Who said it and what movie?"

"What?" I feel dizzy and off balance. Like any minute I could fall.

"It's a line from a movie. What's the movie?"

"I don't know."

"Damn." She snaps her fingers. "I don't either." She puts a hand to her head like she's thinking. "Nope. It's not there." She shakes her head as she walks across the room to the couch. "But that doesn't make any difference. We're still gonna blow this joint." She picks up her coat and stops at the door. "See you tomorrow, Marge. We're blowing this joint."

"Have a nice one," she calls back.

"Come on, Mac." She starts across the office to the other door. "We're out of here."

"Where are we going?"

"Where are we going?" She stops and looks at me like she can't figure out if I'm joking or not. "Didn't I tell you

I'm supposed to help take a bunch of kids over to the mountain today? Like right this minute? Can you believe it?"

No, I can't believe it. I just stand there with my arms folded. She looks at me carefully. "You ski don't you?"

"Yeah."

"Good. Then you can help me. That's what you can do."

"But I'm not skiing this year," I tell her.

"And I haven't skied in ten years."

"But, Mrs. Resnick . . ." She starts out the door without me. "You don't understand . . ." I start after her with a thousand reasons why I'm not skiing. She stops and listens to me, hands on her hips, like she doesn't believe me.

"You mean you'd rather stay inside on a beautiful day and talk to me instead of going out there on that beautiful mountain and skiing?"

"Yeah."

"Okay." She steps back into the office. "We'll stay." Throws her coat over a chair. Picks up the phone and dials a couple of numbers. "Marge? Yeah, it's me. Hey, will you go out and tell Bob I can't make his ski class? Tell him I broke a leg or something." She winks at me like it's our little joke. I look down at the rug. She hangs up. Shakes her head. Then sits down on the couch. And points at an easy chair for me to sit in. I sit down. Sun in my eyes.

"Well, Mac, you may not realize it, but you just saved my life."

"What do you mean?" I squint at her. She never says what you expect. Always has to be something different.

"I hate skiing."

"I don't."

"Oh?" She sounds surprised. "You just got through telling me how much you hated it."

"I lied."

"Oh?" Her green eyes whip right through the sun at me. "Well, if we're going to lie to each other, we're going to have a pretty confusing time."

"Yeah? Well, you lied to me."

"Oh? And how did I do that?"

"All that crap about having to help with skiing. You're just trying to get me out on the mountain skiing. Right? Rosen told you he wanted me out for the ski team, I bet. So you tried to trick me into going out there. I don't need that crap."

"What do you need then?"

"Nothing. I don't need nothing. I don't want nothing. I don't like nothing. And that includes everything and everybody." I stare straight at her. Straight into the sun. Until tears squeeze out of my eyes. "Oh, what's the use?" I get up and start for the door.

"So where are you going?" she calls after me. I turn around. And stare at her flaming red hair.

"Nowhere."

"Sounds good."

"Don't tell me it sounds good. It doesn't sound good."

"So what do we do, Mac?"

"Don't ask me! You're the fucking counselor! You tell me."

"Okay, Mac, I will." She pulls a fat earring out from

under her red hair and studies it. Like it's telling her what to say.

"I think you and I need to talk about some of the things that are bothering you."

"Brilliant," I snarl at her.

"But I don't know what those things are, so I don't even know where to begin. Or what to ask. So I want you to do me a favor."

"What favor?"

"I want you to make a list of questions I should ask you. That way I won't ask the wrong ones. The ones that might make you even madder at me or hurt you."

"Me make a list?" I can't believe this lady.

"Yeah." She says it like it's my idea. "Just jot down some questions."

"Aren't you supposed to figure that out? Isn't that your job?"

"Yeah." She gets up and walks over to the hall door. "But I guess I need your help. To do it right." She opens the door to the hall.

"My help. Who the hell's in charge, anyway?" I growl at her.

"I guess you are, Mac."

· 37 ·

Cooked carrots the color of squash. Slabs of ham floating in thin gravy. Powdered mashed potatoes. It's enough to make me sick. I slide my tray along the stainless steel railing. Grab a couple of tan puddings and a milk. Pay the cashier circled in smoke.

Walk across the cafeteria. Empty except for tables and chairs and a few kids. I slide the pudding off the tray onto an empty table. Drop an empty notebook next to the pudding. I cut civics for this. I pull out a chair and sit down. Rip open the milk and swallow it. Bit by bit.

I got Resnick next period and she wants a list. She even sent a note reminding me. Like I'm an idiot. Like I'm gonna forget. I'm not gonna forget. I might not do it. But I sure as hell ain't gonna forget it. A list? I look at the lines on the blank sheet of paper. Scoop the whipped cream off the top of the pudding. Let it melt on my tongue.

Hardly slept last night. Nightmares like fever dreams. Couldn't stay in bed. Went downstairs. Three o'clock in the morning. The laundry room light falling across the kitchen floor. The dryer door open. I sit down in front of it and stare in. Waiting for night to end. Wondering what happens when you stick your head in a gas dryer.

She wants a list. I've got lists. Lists of homework I'm never going to do. Lists of clothes I'm never going to wear. Lists of kids I never want to see. Lists of sports I'm never going to play. Lists of a thousand things I used to like. But don't anymore. Lists of lists. Like nightmares. But she's not getting any list from me. I look down at the bowls of tan pudding. The empty milk carton. The blank pad of paper.

"Hey, lover boy." A voice crawls across the table at me. I don't have to look up to see Woody's face creeping towards me. "What you doing? Writing love notes?"

"Hey, Mac, is that you?" Brook is right next to him. "Didn't see you in class."

"No kidding."

"What are you writing?" Shawn sits down next to me.

"Nothing." I hold up the pad for everyone to see. "See? Not a damn thing."

"Jesus, Mac, you don't have to hyperventilate." Shawn slides down a couple of chairs. I look at him. The black curls spilling over his forehead. And try to remember. Did I slug him with my right hand or my left? Must be my left, because looking at him makes it ache.

"Hey, twerp, don't be an asshole." Woody sits down across from me.

"So where's your sweet thing?" Brook grabs one of the puddings and starts scooping it into his mouth with his fingers.

"In his pants." Woody looks at me with that stupid smile of his. That belongs on a list all by itself. That smile.

"One of these days, Woody, I'm going to take that stupid smile of yours and stretch it right across the top of this table."

"Holy shit." He leans back in his chair and laughs.

"Just like a goddamn tablecloth."

He laughs even louder.

"Jeez, Mac, you don't have to get so sore." Brook slides the empty bowl back in front of me. "He's just joking."

"Thanks, Brook." I look at him. "You want the other one too?"

"Sure. Why not?"

"Here." I slide it towards him. "But you'd better check it for bugs. I thought I saw one."

"Bugs?" He leans over the bowl. "I don't see any bugs."

"Look closer."

He does. I put my hand on the back of his head and shove his face right into it.

• 38 •

It's not even Friday and the parents are gone. We're sitting on their double bed. Peter's got an old *Time* magazine with Arafat on the cover. And we're looking at pictures of terrorists. What do I tell them about terrorists? About car bombs? About blowing yourself up to bits? Like your life depended on it? How do I tell them that I want to be a terrorist? That I wouldn't mind blowing a few people off the face of this earth? Peter flips the page. And we stare at a bunch of bearded guys. Rifles over their shoulders. Bombs in their pockets.

"I don't want to look anymore." Avery climbs off the bed. Crawls over to the window and peers out between the curtains. Looking for terrorists, I know. But I don't say anything. Because if I do he'll be up all night sitting at the end of my bed. Waiting for the parents to get home. Waiting for the first bomb to strike.

"Avy, there are no terrorists in our country," I try to calm him.

"How do you know?" He crawls back onto the bed.

"I know because they're only in the Middle East."

"Where's that? Boston?"

"Avy." Peter slaps his head. "The Red Sox are in Boston. The Red Sox aren't terrorists, are they, Mac?"

"Jeez, guys. There are no terrorists in Boston. There are no terrorists anywhere near us. They're thousands and thousands of miles away from here."

"Whew." Avery lets out a big sigh. "But what about the Red Sox?"

"They play baseball, guys."

"See, Petey."

"I knew that."

"No, you didn't." Avery makes a face at Peter. Then turns to me. "I'm gonna be a policeman when I grow up, Mac."

"Why?"

"So I can kill terrorists." He karates the magazine out of my hands.

"Hey, watch it, Avery." I reach for the magazine. But before I can grab it, he tears it in half.

"There." He looks at Peter and me like he's just saved our lives.

"You're crazy, Avery." Peter shakes his head. "I'm not going to be a policeman. They get killed."

"So what are you going to be?"

"I'm going to be a dog when I grow up."

"A dog?" I look at Peter real carefully to see if he's joking. He's not. So I break the news to him. "Peter, you can't be a dog when you grow up."

"Why not?"

"It just doesn't happen that way. You have to be born a puppy if you're going to be a dog."

"I can be a dog if I want to."

"Pete." The phone rings. I reach over and pick it up.

"Mac, I got the tickets."

It's Jenny. Oh, Jesus, I've got Jenny on the phone and two crazy brothers on the bed.

"Wait a minute." I put the receiver under my arm. And point to the door. "Time to leave, guys." They don't move. I grab a pillow and hold it over my head. They start slowly out of the room. I get up and shut the door behind them. To make sure they don't sneak up on me I take the phone into the closet and pull the door tight behind me. I finally get the receiver up to my mouth.

"What did you say?"

"I said, I got the tickets."

"For what?" I stare across the dust-covered shoes.

"Dire Straits."

Dire Straits? "For when?"

"Two weeks from Wednesday."

Terrific. Her voice is weak and faint. I try hard to listen. I try hard to remember the rush her voice used to give me. The rush I used to get from Dire Straits. But I can't. How am I going to tell her I don't want to go? That a thousand weeks from Wednesday is too soon. That, like a terrorist, I'm waiting to be blown to bits.

• 39 •

I wake to the sound of the stairs creaking. I open an eye. And over me as far as I can see are clothes hanging from the ceiling. I'm in their closet!

Footsteps circle the landing and stop at the bedroom door. How am I going to get out of this one? I turn my head and listen to the door open. High heels and sneakers step into the room. What am I going to tell them? That I fell asleep while I was on the phone? That I crawled into the closet to get away from Peter and Avery? Kids don't just fall asleep in closets.

"Shhh. Don't . . . you'll wake the kids." My mother's voice is like the soft slap of a hand.

"No, we won't." Dad's voice is a soft whisper I've never heard before.

"Don't, Dan."

The box springs squeak. Oh, no, what is going on here? I hear a sneaker drop to the floor. The high heels follow. I close my eyes and ears.

"Shhh." My mother's voice is soft as the light going off. "The door."

I hear bare feet cross the carpet. The door closes.

"What's wrong now?" My father's voice is still that soft whisper.

"I'm upset. That's all."

"Shhh. About what?"

"I don't know. I'm just really upset. That's all."

"About what?"

"About Mac, I guess." And she starts to cry.

"Mac?" He says my name like it's a pain. "What's wrong with Mac? I mean, he's seeing a counselor, isn't he?"

"He's seeing a counselor, Dan. You make it sound like he's on the honor roll."

"No, I don't. I'm simply stating a fact. He's seeing a counselor. I mean, he is, isn't he?"

"So?"

"So?"

"So I think that's something to worry about."

"Well ... I think it's something not to worry about."

"We obviously have two opinions about it."

"Obviously." My father gets off the bed. I hear him walk across the room to the bathroom. The sound of running water fills the room. "Want a bath?"

"Maybe later. He's just so . . . so sad. We probably shouldn't have asked him to take care of the twins tonight. What's wrong with him, Dan?"

"Nothing. He's just a kid."

"You don't think he's sad?"

"All teenagers are sad. So what's the big deal? It's just a stage."

"He didn't used to be sad." Suddenly my mother's really crying. "He used to be such a wonderful boy."

A wonderful boy. I wipe my eyes. I used to be a wonderful boy.

"He doesn't want a dog," she goes on.

"Who says?"

"He does."

"So come on, Sarah, who cares?"

"I care."

"Why in God's name should the poor kid want a dog?"

"It's symbolic."

"Symbolic? You sound like a college student, for crying out loud. Symbolic of what?"

"Of caring. Of being alive. Of being happy. Mac's not happy, Dan. He's miserable. Does he seem happy to you?"

Dad doesn't answer. Come on, Dad, why the hell don't you answer? Do I seem happy? Do I seem alive? That's my cue to crawl out of this tomb. And show them I'm alive. But I don't move.

"You just forget what it's like to be a teenager. That's all."

"And he's lonely. I think he's really lonely. A dog would be good for him."

"He doesn't need a dog, honey. He needs a girl."

"I thought he had a girl."

I once had a girl.

"Not a regular one. He needs a girl. That's all."

I need a girl.

"That's just what you need."

"You coming in the bath?"

"Maybe." I can hear her roll over on her side. "I sure hope this counselor helps. I hope she can talk to him." She gets off the bed and starts across the carpet for the bathroom. "I can't get two words out of him."

Two words? I try to remember the last two words I said to her. Try, good night, Mother. That's three. But she doesn't hear me. She steps into the bathroom. Closes the door behind her. And the sound of running water drowns out her voice.

I crawl out of the closet. Across the floor and out into the hall. I get to my feet and limp through the night light. Too tired to climb up to my bed. I lie down on the beanbag on Avery and Peter's floor. And stare up at the ceiling.

Their Lego spaceships floating in the dark like stars.

She thinks I need a dog. What the hell does she know? I've got a little brother who wants to be a dog. What the hell do I need another one for? And he thinks I'm fine. Just fine. All I need is a girl.

Right. I'm fine. Just fine.

I shiver in the cold starlight. And pull the green rug up over my shoulders. Waiting for the spaceships to burst into flames.

• 40 •

"I'm sorry we missed each other last week."

I don't answer her.

"I was sick."

I still don't answer.

"Must be something going around."

Must be. I don't look at her. But stare at the folds in the curtains. And beyond. At the gray sky. Like nightfall. Falling down all around us.

"Is it snowing?" She looks over her shoulder out into the grayness. "Sure looks like it." She looks back at me. "Well, I suppose that's enough on the weather. How about if we spend a little time on you?"

I don't answer.

"Well, we could talk about the weather if that's what you prefer."

"You counselors are all the same." My voice is too loud for the room.

"Oh?"

"You all think you're God."

"Is that right?"

"That's right."

"How so?"

"You pretend to be concerned, like you really care. Then you just disappear. You're never around."

"Oh ..." She says it like she thinks. In slow motion. "You feel like I abandoned you."

"I don't feel anything. You have me write up a stupid list. Like you're too dumb to figure stuff out yourself. And then you don't even show. It pisses me off."

"I don't blame you. But Marge sent you a note, didn't she?"

"No, Marge didn't send me a note."

"I'm sorry. I'm really sorry, Mac. She should have."

I don't say anything.

"You sound really angry. Like you feel I've betrayed you."

"I'm getting used to it."

She just looks at me for a while. Like she's really sorry. "So where does that leave us, Mac?"

"You're the counselor."

"Mac, I don't like the way this is going."

"Yeah. Well, I don't either."

"So what do you suggest?"

"I suggest I leave."

"That's getting to be a familiar song."

"Yeah?"

"Yeah. I think we're missing something."

"Try last week."

"I said I was sorry."

"Sure you are. You're just jerking me around. Just like all the other adults you can't trust."

"Mac, I'm not jerking you around."

"They why weren't you here last week? And why do you play all these stupid games with me? Like I'm an idiot. Take me out for breakfast? Try to make me go skiing? Tell me that you like me? You don't like me. You don't even know me."

"I'm getting to know you."

"No, you're not. Nobody knows me."

"I guess it feels that way to you, Mac. But I have a feeling a few people know you. Like your parents, for example."

"Give me a break, will you?"

"You don't think they know you?"

"No. They don't know me."

"What is it that they don't know about you?"

"You're the counselor. You tell me."

"Is your mother working?"

"What difference does that make? My mother wants to buy me a dog. That's how deep she goes. Everything will be fine if Mac has a dog. She thinks I'm eight years old. That's how well she knows me."

"And your father?"

"I'm not talking about my father. My father's a faggot. All he wants to talk about is adolescence. An adolescent is this. An adolescent is that. And everything's fine. Always fine. He thinks I'm just fine."

"But you don't."

"Don't what?"

"Think you're fine."

"No. I'm not fine. Can't you see?"

"I can see you're really hurt, Mac. I can see something or somebody's really hurt you."

"Nobody's hurt me. Nobody touches me."

"I mean your feelings, Mac. Something or someone's done a number on you."

"I don't want to talk about this."

"About being hurt?"

"I said, I don't want to talk about it."

"Okay. But sometimes it's painful to talk about hurt, Mac."

"Can't you leave it alone?"

"No, I can't, Mac. But I'll try to talk in ways you feel okay about. I think —"

"I said, I don't want to hear what you think."

"I just have this sense, Mac, that more than your feelings have been hurt."

"No."

"And I need to ask you some questions —"

"No." I put my hands over my ears.

"To help us understand —"

"Mrs. Resnick," I yell, "I said no."

"Oh, Mac," she whispers, "it's never easy. Maybe we should take a break now. But I want to see you first thing tomorrow."

"What if I don't want to see you?"

"Would you like to see someone else?"

"What if I did?"

"Well, maybe right now that might not be a bad idea, Mac. Maybe you should talk with a counselor who's a man. Maybe there are some things that you —"

"I'm not talking with Cartledge."

"No. I was thinking of someone else, Mac. Someone who I think you'll really like. What do you think?"

I don't think anything. And she just sits back on the couch and looks at me with those green eyes of hers. I look away. Out the window. At the first snowflakes burning holes in the dark.

• 41 •

Noise like jet airplanes. A black railing in front of us we hold on to. Twenty thousand other kids around us. Waiting for Dire Straits. In the Cage. The whole basketball court a stage. Hoops drawn up to the ceiling. Speakers taller than backboards. Blacker than graves.

We're buried halfway up the bleachers. Campus cops in green uniforms cruise below us looking for trouble. Walkie-talkies pressed to their ears. Lights flash on and off. Turning us red and gold. I look at Jenny. She smiles that smile of hers that used to take my breath away. And leans towards me. I stare out across the darkness in between the flashes of light.

"Here, man." A hand passes me a skinny cigarette. I know what it is. I pass it on to Jenny. She takes a sniff and looks at me. Smiles and passes it along.

Concerts are just like everything else. You wait around for them. And wait around for them. And you think you know what they're going to be like. And then they finally come. And they're nothing like you thought they were going to be. Nothing.

It's nearly nine-thirty before they show. When they finally get on stage they glow in the dark. One of them grabs a microphone like he's going to dance with it. And just like that the music starts. Loud enough to blow us away. And twenty thousand kids cheer like it's the end of the world. You can barely hear a thing. Jenny pushes her leg against mine, keeping time with the music. I look away. The bass guitar rolls through the noise like headlights in heavy traffic. And twenty thousand kids shut up. Cymbals gentle as rain. Sheets of lead guitar. Falsetto harmony. And then the lead voice sadder than life.

> *Here I am again in this mean old town.*
> *And you're so far away . . .*
> *So far I just can't see . . .*
> *So far away from me.*

I turn and look at Jenny. She's looking off at center stage. Dire Straits. Lights flashing. Legs and arms sparkling. Guitars dancing.

> *I get so tired when I have to explain*
> *When you're so far away from me . . .*
> *So far I just can't see.*

She turns and looks at me. Tears like earrings hang from her eyes. I turn away and stare off into the faces of twenty thousand other kids. Broken by colored strobe lights. How can I explain? She's so far away from me. What makes a kid like me? So far away. Like I just don't care. I hold on to the edge of the bleacher seat. Like I'm blasting off into outer space. When I dare to look down, she's a thousand miles away. Just a speck among twenty thousand faces. And Dire Straits is driving me farther and farther out. Until I'm so far away I know I'll never make it back.

• 42 •

Mrs. Bosworth is drinking coffee from a Styrofoam cup. Brook and Shawn are playing dot-square. Like they do every homeroom. It's overcast and cold. Didn't want to get out of bed. Too tired from the concert. Woke up in the middle of the night again. Sweaty and cold. Same dream. The guy in the white coat standing over me. This time whispering in my ear. Somebody's hurt you. Somebody's hurt you. Until I got out of bed and went downstairs. And stared at the front of the kitchen stove.

"Game," Brook shouts.

"Another one," Shawn shouts back. Jabbing little dots across the paper.

"Mac." A hand touches my shoulder. I turn and Mrs. Resnick is standing beside me. Like in a dream. I'm almost glad to see her. "How about a cup of coffee?"

I look at her and then at Mrs. Bosworth. Who smiles like it's a conspiracy. So I follow her down the aisle. Out into the empty hall. No one is in the waiting room either. She pours two cups of coffee. Hands me one. Takes the other. And walks into her office. I follow her over to the couch where she sits down.

"Well, Mac." Her voice is so soft I can barely hear her. "I'm sorry to pull you out of homeroom."

"That's okay," I whisper back.

"I was worried about you. And just wanted to make sure that you had a chance to talk with someone this morning."

My eyes drop to the carpet. Suddenly I'm cold. Chills whistle along my spine like wind. I can hear my heartbeat. Somebody's hurt you. Somebody's hurt you. Somewhere in the distance Mrs. Resnick is still talking.

". . . and you're absolutely right that there are some things you and I just won't be comfortable talking about . . ."

Like bad dreams that keep you up all night.

". . . like issues of sex. And sexual identity."

All they can think about is sex. Even crazy red-haired ladies want to think about sex.

"So I've asked . . ."

Somebody's hurt you. Somebody's hurt you.

". . . a colleague of mine to meet with you this morning."

Up all night. Staying away from bad dreams.

". . . a friend of mine."

Is no friend of mine.

". . . in the waiting room. Ah, yes, here he is. Come in. Come in."

Come in. Yeah. Everybody come in. Somebody's hurt you. Somebody's hurt you. Bring 'em all in. Bring in the whole fucking school. Bring in the whole fucking country. We're talking sex.

"... is Mac. Mac, this is Dr. Amidon."

"Good morning, Mac."

Good morning, Dr. America. Hurt is in the eye of the beholder. Somebody's hurt you. Nobody's hurt me. Nobody.

"... I've got some things to type up. So I'll wait in the other room."

Leaving. Just like a counselor. Just like all the rest. I watch her. Walk right out the door. And close it behind her. Bailing out. Leaving me. Alone with Dr. America. Good morning, Dr. America. But you'll have to excuse me. Somebody's hurt you. Nobody's hurt me. I've gotta go. I start after her.

"Mrs. Resnick."

"... Mac. Come sit down. She'll be back in a minute." A voice like water. Running after me. Flooding the office.

"Mac." Suddenly he's in front of me. His face. Out of focus.

"Mrs. Resnick, I changed my mind. I want to talk with you." I want to run after her. But I can't move. Somebody's hurt you. Somebody's hurt you. I turn away. And stare at a glass cabinet in the corner of the room. I don't remember the cabinet. Or the scale. Or the smell of alcohol. But that face. Even out of focus I remember that face. It's the fucking doctor.

"Mac." His face is on top of me.

"Mac." His breath is on my neck.

"Mac." His arm is around me.

"Take your fucking arm off me," I scream. *"Mrs. Resnick."* Somebody's hurt you.

"Mrs. Resnick ... come back ... please, come back."
Somebody's hurt me.

• 43 •

"Mac." Her face floats over me like a light.

"Mac, it's all right. I'm here. I'm here." A hand under my neck pulls lightly. "You feel like getting up?" And the room spins around. Ceiling to floor. My head aches. My teeth ache.

"I want to go home."

"Sit on the couch and rest first." The windows glide towards us. The couch slides under my legs. Something warm settles over me. I look down. A red parka is spread over my legs. She sits somewhere near me. Her voice like eggshells. Somebody's hurt you.

"It's time for us to talk, Mac."

I stare down across the red folds of the parka. Like a sunset. Red hills I want to climb into and disappear. A red desert.

"Mac." I look across the red sand. Her green eyes the tops of palm trees. "You listening?"

One way or the other. Somebody's hurt you. I look across the sand. If I start right now it'll take me a lifetime to get out of here.

"Mac." The green eyes flash in the wind. I've got to go. But which way? Which way do I go? I turn and look out the window. At the red mountain. The red parking lot.

"Mac."

130

Somebody is standing out there. In the parking lot. With a white jacket on. But no pants. He doesn't have any pants on. The doctor doesn't have any pants on! He looks up at the window. And starts walking across the parking lot. Right towards me.

"He doesn't have any pants on," I scream.

"Who, Mac?"

"Mrs. Resnick," I scream. She lands next to me. I grab her hand. "The bastard doesn't have any pants on. It's him. It's him."

"It's who, Mac?"

"The doctor," I scream. "The fucking doctor."

"Which doctor?"

"He's coming over here."

"No, he's not, Mac."

"Yes, he is. He is." I watch him snaking between the cars. Heading right for us. He curls around the back of a red Honda. And stares up at the window. Right at us. Somebody's hurt you.

"Mrs. Resnick," I scream. Somebody's hurt you.

"Mac." A hand floats through the air towards me. It lands against my face. My head jerks back. My face stings. The doctor stops smiling. And shakes a fist at me. Another hand grabs my chin. And spins my head around. A soft face with freckles.

"Mac." The hand pulls my head against her soft shoulder. And I cry. "It's all right, Mac. Shhh. He's gone. I promise you. I'm here. To help you get rid of him."

"He's out there right now."

"Where, Mac?" she whispers. "Show me."

"In the parking lot." I feel her move to look out the window.

"No one's there, Mac. Look for yourself. What's scaring you is just in your head."

I turn and look. The parking lot is empty except for cars. The red Honda is gone. I turn away and look down at my lap. The parka is too hot around my legs. My back is dripping with sweat. I kick the parka to the floor and start to stand up. She pushes me back down.

"Here." She hands me a can of Coke. "Take a sip."

It burns my lips. And the back of my throat. I swallow it. Bit by bit.

"How's that? Better?" I don't know what she means. "I have to go."

"In a minute, Mac. Just rest." She takes the can of Coke out of my hand and puts it on the floor. "I bet you wish this would all go away. I bet you've been trying your hardest to make it all go away. It's tough work, though, isn't it, Mac? I mean it's impossible work. Holding everything in. It must be driving you crazy."

I look across the blue and brown squares of her skirt. Sweat like bombs dropping off my spine. I listen for the explosions. Somebody's hurt you.

"Somebody's really hurt you, Mac ... worse than I thought."

The skirt is wool. Like a blanket.

"The doctor did things to you he shouldn't have."

"What?" My voice an explosion.

"He touched you in ways he shouldn't have."

"What?"

"He touched your private parts."

"What do you take me for?" I scream. "A faggot?"

"No, I don't."

"Yes, you do." I try to get up. But she grabs my hand. "Will you let go of me?" I scream.

"Listen to me, Mac."

"Let go of me."

"Mac."

"I said, let go of me."

"Mac. What this doctor did is wrong. I mean, it's so wrong that it's against the law. Do you know what it's called, Mac? Sexual assault. That's what it's called. And do you know something else? He can go to jail for doing what he did to you."

"I don't want to talk about it."

"I don't either, Mac. But I have to tell you something. By law I have to file a 51-A. Do you know what that means?"

I shake my head.

"That means I have to let the Department of Social Services know what happened to you."

"I don't want them to know."

"I don't blame you, Mac, but it's a law. And it's a law designed to protect you."

"It's a shitty law."

"I'm sure it seems that way to you right now, but it's a good law if it protects good kids like you from bad adults."

"Yeah? Well, I don't care."

"Well, I care, Mac. And part of my caring is to let people who love you and who will care for you know what has happened."

"No!" I yell. "You're not telling them and you're not telling my parents."

"We have to tell your parents, Mac. I'm not letting you leave me or this school today without your parents coming to take care of you."

"Take care? Bullshit. They'll just think I'm a faggot. Just like you do."

"I think nothing of the kind. And they won't either. Being gay or not being gay has nothing to do with what happened to you. Do you understand that, Mac? You were sexually assaulted by a man. That doesn't make you gay. But it does make you a victim of assault." She clears her throat. "I know it's really hard for you to trust adults now, Mac, but I want you to try to really trust me for the next few hours. Starting right now, when I tell you that your parents are going to love and care for you —"

"No, they're not."

"More than they ever have."

"I don't want to tell them."

"I'll tell them for you."

• 44 •

"There you are, Mac." I turn around and Mr. Rosen is walking towards me. "Your parents are here, talking with

134

Mrs. Resnick. Do you mind if I walk down that way with you?"

He knows. What am I going to say? What's he gonna say? He stops at the drinking fountain.

"Want a drink?" He points towards the fountain like it's just been installed or something. I'm not thirsty. But I take a drink. Tastes like rusted pipes. I back away and he smiles at me. Like he just gave me the world or something. Then he takes a long drink.

"Mac." He wipes his mouth and steps towards me. I back away. He clears his throat. Water dripping off of his chin. Somebody's hurt you.

"I just want to tell you . . ."

Sure. I back up farther. He moves towards me. I watch his feet. Black shoes. With black tassels. That fly through the air like black birds when he walks. I back away. Trying to remember the blackbird rhyme. Somebody's hurt you.

". . . how sorry . . . about what you've been through . . . doesn't help you to hear this . . ."

Baked in a pie.

". . . just wanted you to know . . ."

Four and twenty blackbirds.

". . . how much we all care about you."

When the pie was opened.

". . . care about you."

Bullshit. He shuffles his feet. All the blackbirds fly away.

"So what about those Celtics?"

I glance up at him to see what I missed. Not much. He's still smiling. And we start down the hall like we're headed for the Garden.

"Think Bird will have triples?" The tassels dance along his feet.

"Depends where they come down." My voice flies in from somewhere near the ceiling.

"Mr. Rosen," Marge calls from across the hall, "Resnick's been waiting for this young man for fifteen minutes."

"My fault." Mr. Rosen steps quickly towards the office. Then turns to me. "I'm really sorry, Mac. If there's anything . . ."

I don't say anything. I walk into the office and Marge is at her desk. The typewriter's on. The phone's half off the hook. Her desk a mess of forms.

"Go on in." She waves her fat arm at me. "They're waiting for you."

The door is closed. I stand there.

"Go in, Mac. I tell you they're waiting for you."

"Yeah?" I turn and look at her. She licks her thumb. Going through her forms like a mess of cards.

"Would I lie to you?"

· 45 ·

I open the door and walk slowly into Resnick's office. The room is filled with sunlight. I look down towards the couch. They're all sitting there. Shadow and light.

"Come in, Mac." Mrs. Resnick stands. But I don't move. I stand there. Squinting into the sun. Father and Mother. Sports coat and tie. All smiles. Skin tight around cheekbones. My jaw aches. My brain borderline.

"Mac?" She glides out of the light. Her face dark. Her hair on fire. "Why don't you sit in this chair next to me. I don't think the sun will be in your eyes. If it is I'll pull the curtain."

I sit down in the folding chair. Curl my feet around it. Just in case. My mother lets out a long sigh. My father winks at me.

". . . just getting to know your parents . . . now I know why you're such a neat kid."

My parents mumble something dumb. And look stupid. I stare straight into the sun. Wanting to blind myself. When I look at them they're broken up by sunspots.

"All of us are very worried about Mac." She looks at me through the sunspots. Her green eyes shining. "Why a kid with so much going for him . . . down the tubes . . . makes no sense."

"No sense." They shake their heads in bits and pieces.

"Something traumatic has happened to him . . . so painful that . . . pretended it never happened . . . pushed it right out of his mind . . . no easy task . . . because it doesn't work."

A spot drifts across her face. And she disappears. Except for her mouth. That keeps talking.

". . . just doesn't work . . . but he tried on one level to deny that this terrible thing happened, but on other levels,

137

daily life for example . . . impossible for him to cope with."
Her face floats out from under one spot. Her eyes shine
straight at me. Before they go under again.

"What terrible thing? What are you talking about?"
His voice from across the room too loud. Like he wants to
scream. "Mac tells us everything."

Sure. Everything. Everything. Somebody's hurt me.
Somebody's hurt me. Can't you see that? Do I have to
spell out everything for you?

"Some things kids can't talk about."

"What things?" Her voice choking. "What?" Her face
drifts out of the light. Like a mask. Her hands twisted together. "You make it sound so awful."

"Because it is awful." I stare back into the sun. "What
I'm about to tell you . . . extremely serious . . ." Like it's an
eraser. Or an eclipse. Blots everything out.

"Just tell us!" His voice slams up against me. I look towards him. His face is impossible to see. The sun is on his
shoulders.

"Your son has been sexually assaulted."

"Sexually what?"

"Assaulted."

"How is that possible?" He swings towards me. "Mac?"

"Mac." My mother rises out of her seat. Past him. Her
face suddenly at my knees. Her cold hands take my hands.
Her sad face. Melting. Blue make-up running down her
cheeks. I try to block her out. I try to remember the
rhyme. Her eyes open. They begin to sing. He's gay. Hey,
the kid is gay. Her cold fingers touch my face. Like ice.

Mother, don't touch me. You shouldn't touch me. Somebody's hurt you. Somebody's hurt me.

"Trust us?" She holds my face in her hands. "Please, trust us, darling. You've been so brave."

"Mac." My father steps out of the sun. And, wrapping his huge arms around us, weeps. For the first time in my life.

• 46 •

She stands up like the meeting's over. My parents stand, too. The sun's left the room. "There are a few other things I have to say to you." She runs a hand through her hair. "As I told Mac this morning, maybe the hardest thing for him to get over will be the feeling that somehow this was his fault. It wasn't. You know that, and I know that. We just have to convince Mac of that. And I'm going to tell this to Mac every time I see him. It's not his fault. It's not his fault. It's never the child's fault. Never." They nod their heads. I look out the window. It's getting dark. The sun's burned out.

"Kids who have been sexually assaulted are no different from rape victims. A woman who's been raped is going to feel just like you, Mac. Like it was her fault. That the only reason she was raped was because there was something wrong with her. Well, I have news for you, Mac. There was nothing wrong with her. And there's nothing wrong with you. She would have been raped no matter who she was, or what she was feeling or thinking. It's the same with the man who raped you. What you were thinking or feeling was totally irrelevant. Do you understand? It could have happened to anybody, Mac. In fact, there probably have been other kids assaulted." She stops talking.

"I've gone on more than I intended. I just feel so strongly that for a kid to get sexually assaulted is bad enough without all this guilt. Just remember it wasn't your fault. It's never the child's fault. You understand?" She looks right at my parents. "We'll tell him that every night and every morning. Until he believes us."

She starts for the door. We follow. My mother's arm around my shoulder. In the hall she stops and stands to the side. My parents shake hands with her. As I start to leave she snags my hand.

"You have a special son here," she says to them.

Bullshit. I pull away. Quickly. So she can't see my eyes. And run down the empty hall and out into the cold night.

· THREE ·

47

I wake up with the moon shining in my face. The March wind howls against the house. The windows whistle. I roll out of bed and look down across the white fields. Galvanized buckets, ripped off the sides of maple trees, wheel across the old snow. Without a sound. I get back in bed. Pull the covers over my face. And try to remember. A dream. Like a good feeling I once had.

"Mac?" Peter is standing at the door wearing his blue sweat suit.

"What?" He's supposed to be in bed. It's ten-thirty at night. The parents are out. I'm lying on their bed. Talking on the phone to Brook.

"Can I be your dog?"

"What?"

"Can I be your dog?"

"Petey." I cover the phone with my hand and whisper, "No, you can't be my dog. I told you a hundred times, you're not a dog."

"Then Avery can't be one either."

"That's right. Now get out of here."

He doesn't listen to me. But drops down to his hands and knees and barks at my feet.

"Peter, cut that out."

I might as well be talking to a dog. He bites the top of my sock and shakes his head.

"Cut it out," I hiss, "or I'll slug you." But what do I know? One minute it's just Peter pulling on my foot. The next minute Avery's there. And both of them are ripping my socks to shreds.

"Mac? What's that?" Brook asks.

"Nothing," I lie. "Just a couple of neighbors' dogs that broke in to the house. Hold on a minute." I push the phone under the pillow. There's only one thing I can do. I've got to be a real jerk. I stand up and start for the door.

"Come on, pups," I call. "Come on. Good dogs."

"Woof."

"Woof." They let go of my socks and start following. Out the door. Down the hall. And into their room. Wagging their rear ends like they have tails.

"Good dogs. Up. Up," I call when we get to their beds. And smack the mattress with my hand. "Up."

They spring up onto their beds. Their tails wagging. Their tongues hanging out of their mouths. I pat them on their heads.

"Good dogs. Time to go to sleep." They whine a little. Crawl in tight circles. Then curl up next to their pillows. I pull their comforters over their chins. They look up at me with big, doglike eyes. I don't know how they do it. I pat them on their heads again. Whisper good night. Turn off the lights and tiptoe out of the room backwards.

"Mac, hug. Hug," one of them barks.

Hug. Hug. There's no end to it. I go back to their beds and hug each one. And start back out of the room.

"Thanks, Mac," Peter calls.

"Love you, Mac."

"Yeah," I call back over my shoulder. "Love you."

• 49 •

I lie in bed listening to the Talking Heads. The record turning round and round makes circles of light on the ceiling. I listen to the words, but don't hear them. Just the music. Up there on the ceiling. Thinking about yesterday. How Resnick drove me down to Springfield.

"Where are we going?" I asked her.

"To talk to some other kids who've experienced sexual violence." She said it like we were going to a movie or something.

We drive up to some school looking building. Inside there are these carpeted halls. And this room with mirrors for blackboards. And two kids. One's kind of big with black, curly hair. And pockmarks. The other kid's shorter than me. Blond hair. A milk-colored mustache. Mrs. Resnick and some guy with glasses and a beard sit in with us. We talk a long time. About all kinds of stuff. But mostly about sexual assault. I don't talk much. But these two guys do. The big kid, Patrick, talks mostly about how angry he got. How he was going to kill the guy. Until he realized it wasn't his fault. That the guy was sick. That it could have happened to anybody.

"Now I can live with it." He nods his big head slowly.

"You mean you don't want to kill the guy anymore?" the kid with the mustache asks.

"I didn't say that." The big kid looks at Resnick. Then me. "I still want to kill him. But I ain't gonna."

"Why?" Resnick asks.

"I don't want to get my ass fried. Just for some sicko."

"No. Me either." The little guy pulls at his mustache.

Mrs. Resnick looks at him. "What about you, Vinny? How did you feel?"

"Me?" He holds a thumb up to his chest. "I don't know. A lot like Pat, you know?" He looks down at the floor. "I would have killed the bastard if I could, I was so mad. Real mad at myself, too, you know? Like I did something to make it happen. Took me a long time to figure that one out. You know? That it wasn't my fault. That I wasn't queer. Took me a long time to get over that feeling. Like how could any girl, you know, ever like me." He looks up from the floor. Glances around the room.

"Do they?" The words are out of my mouth before I think them.

"Do they what?" His eyes settle on me.

"I, ah, just wondered if . . . you know."

"If girls like Vinny?" Patrick laughs out loud. "You kidding? They love him. Don't they, Vinny?"

Vinny shrugs. "Sort of."

"Sort of! He's the most popular guy in East Springfield."

"What about you?" I ask Patrick.

"Me?" He sucks air in through his nose. "Me, I'm not like Vinny. I only got one girlfriend. But that's fine for me." He looks at me out of the corner of his eye. "What about you?"

146

"Me?" I shrug my shoulders.

"Yeah, you."

"I'm too young," I lie.

"Bullshit." Vinny and Patrick speak together.

The Heads have reached the end of the record. The needle clicks against the groove. What about you? What about you? I listen to the clicking. And watch the reflection on the ceiling. What about me? What about me? I don't know. I don't know.

It took us an hour to drive home. And not once did Resnick ask me about girls.

Next time it's going to be different. I turn off the stereo. Hang the earphones over the back of my bed. Next time I'm going to talk about girls. Whether she likes it or not.

• 50 •

Fifth period I have computer. Mr. Lindgren. A skinny guy with a beard. Running from computer to computer. Like he's training for the marathon. Always saying, No, no, not like that, like this. And before he can show you, he's racing off to the next computer. Shouting, No, no, not like that. Woody says BASIC has Lindgren by the balls. I don't know. I think he'd be running around no matter what he's teaching.

It's quiet today. He's been out of the room a lot talking to some salesman or something. So the kids are taking advantage of it. Working with the computers while he's gone. There are twenty Apples in the room. Five rows of four. I sit in the back row. Playing Lode Runner. Drilling holes and trying to capture the bad guys. Not thinking about anything. Until the bell rings.

Usually everyone races for the door at once. But today, with things so quiet, we're still working on the computers when the next class comes in. Some kid comes and stands behind my chair. Waiting for me to leave. So I finally flip off the machine. Grab my book bag and head for the door. I'm just coming around the corner when I see her walk into the second row. I can tell it's her by her black hair. I just stop. And don't move. I can feel blood pumping through my forehead. I can hear Patrick's voice. Like it's in the next row. "What about you? You got a girlfriend?"

I haven't seen her since the concert. So I just stand there. Like an idiot. Staring at the blank screen of a computer. Like I'm studying it. Wondering, what am I going to do? Should I go up to her and say hi? Or should I pretend that I don't see her?

Or should I lie? I could say I was sitting there and left my book. And I'm coming back to get it. I start down the aisle and turn into the second row. She's at the very end. Her back to me. Her hair blacker than I remember. Silkier too. I tap her on the shoulder.

"Excuse me, Jenny." The words crawl out of my mouth. "Did I leave a book here?"

"What?" A girl I've never seen turns and looks at me.

"Ah ..." The bell rings. I'm late for civics. The door closes. Mr. Lindgren runs into the room at a hundred miles an hour.

"Program number three. I want to see program number

three." He charges down the front row until he sees me. "Mac, what the hell are you doing here?"

"I, ah, forgot something."

"Well, get it and get out of here. We've got to run program number three."

"Yes, sir."

"What did you forget?" The girl looks at me.

"Ah . . . nothing." I back down the aisle. And out of the room. "Nothing." And sprint down the hallway. My face on fire. Like a total jerk. I can already hear Mrs. Miller. She'll smile and say something really sarcastic like, "Late for class, Mac?"

· 51 ·

Marge is sitting behind her gray desk. Earphones strapped to her head. Typing like crazy. Except when she stops to swear under her breath. But I hear her all the way across the room. So it's no secret when she makes a mistake. Especially when she rips off the earphones. And jams them in a drawer.

"That is quite enough of that." She looks over at me through her big glasses. I look around to see if she's talking to somebody else. But there's no one else in the room.

"Of what?" I ask.

"Enough of that stupid dictation. Excuse me, but . . ." She leans across the top of her desk. So that the green blotter disappears under her huge blouse. She cups her hands to her mouth. And whispers. ". . . but personally I think dictation is a waste of time." She nods her head and stares at me to make sure I've heard what she said. "I mean, blah, blah this . . . blah, blah that." She pushes herself back into her chair. "A person can only take so much." She swivels around so she's facing the typewriter. Grabs the piece of paper. Yanks it out of the carriage. Crumples it between her fists. And throws it in the waste-basket. Then she swivels back towards me.

"Now, Mac, how long have you been waiting?"

"I don't know. Ten minutes."

"That all? In that case, it might be another ten. So make yourself at home." She takes a magazine out of her IN box. And thumbs through it. I reach down and retie one of my laces. When I sit up Marge is looking over her magazine at me.

"So what have you got to say?" she asks.

"Nothing." I shrug.

"Nothing?" She shakes her head slowly. "That's what all you kids say. It's a wonder these counselors ever get a word out of you."

• 52 •

She puts the book down and smiles at me. Sun streaming through her hair. Falling around her shoulders like a shawl.

"So what have you been up to all week?"

"Nothing."

"Nothing special?"

"Why?"

"Just wondering." She puts the book on the floor. "Before I forget, Mac . . . remember I told you that the D.A.'s office is going to send someone out here in a few weeks to get your testimony on tape?"

"Yeah?"

"I thought I should sit in on that. What do you think?"

"I don't know."

"Is that okay with you?"

"I guess."

"Then we can meet here in my office. All right?"

"Okay."

"So, anything exciting happen to you this week?"

"No."

"Anything you want to talk about?"

No. I lie. And look down at my Casio, watching the seconds add up. Thinking it's a good thing they start over at sixty. Otherwise they'd be spilling off my wrist. Running out of time. Making a mess. Wherever I go. Like looking for Jenny in a computer class she never took.

"Mac? You here today?"

I look up from my wrist. And stare right into those green eyes. Yeah, I'm here. And what I want to know is, "Are we ever going to see those guys again?"

"What guys?"

"You know. Vinny and Patrick."

"Sure, we can see them again." She looks down at her skirt. Like she's seen enough of me. "They seem like really together guys."

"Yeah."

"Like they've really worked through a lot of things."

"Yeah," I mumble.

"Was there something they talked about that you'd like to talk about, Mac?"

"Like what?"

"Well, they talked about feelings of anger and hurt and confusion. You seem a little angry this morning. Is that what you'd like to talk about?"

"No," I almost shout.

"They also talked about girlfriends. Is that something you'd like to talk about?"

"So what if it is?"

"Then maybe we should talk about it."

"What if I don't want to?"

"Then we can just sit here."

What a pain in the ass she is. Looking at me like I'm a jerk. Until I say something.

"I thought I saw Jenny the other day."

"We haven't talked about Jenny before."

"No."

"She's a friend?"

"Sort of."

"She was a friend before you were assaulted?"

"Sort of."

"You were going out with her?"

"Sort of."

"What does that mean?"

"What do you mean, what does it mean? It means we sort of went out, that's what it means." It means we sort of liked each other. It means we sort of kissed and stuff.

That's what it means. I kick my book bag across the floor. For crying out loud, why is she so dumb?

"It's hard for you to talk about this, isn't it, Mac?"

"So what if it is? Big deal."

"It is a big deal. It shows how strong you've grown. To be able to tell me about Jenny. I bet you really enjoyed being with her."

"So what if I did?"

"After being assaulted, I bet things changed between you and Jenny."

"Maybe they did."

"And the other day you saw Jenny. What happened?"

"Nothing happened. It wasn't her."

"Who was it?"

"A total stranger. I said hi to a total stranger. Like a total jerk."

"That must have been embarrassing."

"No kidding."

"Well, could you just think of it as practice?"

"What do you mean, practice?"

"Well, you went up to a girl you thought was Jenny. Said hi. And you're still alive to talk about it. When you see the real Jenny, just think how much easier it'll be."

"Yeah, sure."

"I'll bet you a Coke it will be." She stands up and starts across the room to the door. Like the session's over. I grab my book bag and just stand there. Like it's not over.

"Is there something else you want to say, Mac?"

"Yeah."

"I'm listening."

"Do you think, you know . . . that I could like Jenny again?"

"Oh, Mac." She makes a face. "What a tough question. I wish I could answer it for you, but I can't. You're just going to have to wait and see. Sometimes these things take a long time to heal. It just depends."

"Depends on what?"

"How soon you can forgive."

"Forgive who, dammit?"

"Forgive yourself, Mac, and give yourself a break."

"Some help you are."

"I'm sorry . . ." She keeps talking. But I don't hear her. Because I storm right past her. Out into the hall. Like I'm never coming back.

· 53 ·

I can smell the bacon from under my pillow. I pull my head out and look at the clock. Not even half-past six and still dark. I pull the covers up over my head. Try and go back to sleep. But there's no getting away from that smell. By the time I shower and dress and get downstairs it's cooling on a brown paper bag. And he's cooking French toast in the grease.

"I thought that might wake you."

"Didn't," I lie. I hate it when he thinks he knows how to control me. Like all he has to do is press a button here and I'm brushing my teeth. Or a button there and I'm doing my homework. Gets so a guy can't do anything without him saying, I knew you'd be doing that. "I was already up," I tell him, "finishing some homework."

"Thought you might be doing that," he says, dipping a piece of white bread in the eggs.

"I mean I was reading comics." I look at him hard, but he's watching the yellow egg drip off the bread. Then he drops it in the bacon grease. It bubbles and hisses around the egg. So the egg curls up like a fist. I'd like to take a fist right to his head. But I don't. I wait to hear what he's going to say next.

"I said I was reading comics."

"I thought you might."

"Sure you did. Well, I wasn't. I was sleeping. And this stinking bacon woke me up."

"Want some?" He stabs a fat piece with his fork. And holds it up to me. I take it.

"How is it?" He's smiling like he's the morning sunshine or something.

"A little rubbery," I say, breaking off a piece in my mouth. Actually, it's crumbly.

"I thought it was crumbly, too." Smiling like he's a mind reader. He lifts up the edge of the French toast with the fork. Peeks under it. Lets it drop and goes to the icebox. Takes out the orange juice and hands it to me.

"Fill the juice glasses on the table, will you?" He's still smiling. I want to pour the whole carton over his head.

"What's so funny?" I ask. "I missed the joke."

"No joke."

"So why are you Chuckles the Clown this morning?"

"Very funny."

"You want me to pour this over your head?" I hold the orange juice up in the air. "Tell me what's so funny. Why do you have to smile every second?"

"Am I smiling every second?"

"Are you smiling every second? You haven't stopped smiling since I came downstairs. It's pissing me off."

"Well, excuse me." He stops smiling. "If I thought it was pissing you off, I wouldn't be smiling."

"Sure." I don't believe him. Not for a second. He knows how to piss me off. Just standing there and smiling like a jerk. He knows what he's doing.

"Morning." My mother comes sailing through the kitchen, her high heels clicking after her, and goes into the bathroom. With her hair dryer blaring, she yells to Dad about supper. He hands me a plate of steaming French toast. Drops a piece of bacon across the top. I sit down at the table. Put a pad of butter on the toast and while it melts take a gulp of orange juice. I'm halfway through when she sits down next to me. A cup of coffee in front of her. Her hair feathered back across her ears.

"Coffee?" He slides a cup in front of me. And sits down across from me with his own cup. Steam spiraling into the air. I add some milk. Take a sip. And feel it running down the back of my throat. No one's talking. I put the cup down. Look at Dad. He's looking at me. I look at Mum. She's looking at me too. The other kids aren't up yet. And it's so quiet I can hear the bubbler from the fish tank in the next room.

"What's going on?"

"A quiet breakfast," my mother answers. "Kind of peaceful. Just us."

"Why are you guys smiling all the time? It's driving me crazy."

"It's just nice to have you back. That's all."

"What are you talking about, back? I haven't been away."

"Well ..." He speaks slowly. "You've kind of been away, in a sort of hell. And it means a lot to me and Mum to have you safely back. Even if it means you're going to disagree with me on everything."

"Yeah? Well, I'm not disagreeing."

· **• 54 •**

I'm sitting in the back of English not listening to Mrs. Bosworth's sure-fire way to diagram a sentence. Instead of taking notes I'm drawing circles inside the circles. Thinking of skipping town. I've got to see Resnick tomorrow and do that testimony. The bell rings. Everyone slams their books closed and stands up. But Mrs. Bosworth is still talking.

"I have excused no one." She doesn't raise her voice to be heard. We all stare at her. She sweeps her book through the air. Like it's a wand or something. And we sit back down.

"Now, please open your books to page one twelve." We open our books. "Now, class, you may close your books. And you may be excused." Everyone slams their books closed again. And stands up and starts rushing for the door. Except me. I'm still drawing circles.

"Well, I'm glad someone has manners." Mrs. Bosworth looks stiffly at me. Throws her cape over her shoulder and walks out of the room. By the time I get out into the hall she's gone. I walk slowly towards my locker. Past the old Coke machine sweating outside the janitor's room. I drop my book bag in the bottom of my locker and grab a brown bag off the top shelf. Two Cheez Whiz sandwiches with bacon. An apple and a handful of raisins and peanuts. I kick the locker closed. Feel in my pocket for change. And pull out four quarters. I'm rich. I stop at the Coke machine. Drop two of the quarters in the slot. Pull open the skinny glass door and pull out a Mountain Dew. I let the door snap closed. Stick the bottle in the opener and push down. The cap snaps off. The soda fizzes. I put the bottle up to my lips. And take a gulp.

"How can you drink that?" I stop drinking and turn around. She's standing right there behind me. Her hands on her hips.

"What's wrong with this?"

"Junk. That's what's wrong with it."

"Sorry." I back out of her way. "We can't all be perfect."

"You're telling me." She steps past me. Puts her quarters in the machine and pulls out a Diet Coke. Snaps off the cap. And takes a sip.

"So is that any better?"

"This?" She holds up the bottle so I can see it. "This is the drink of cover girls. Don't you know anything?"

"I guess not."

"I guess not." She turns the words around so they're angry. And starts down the hall alone. I watch her go at first. Then I start after her slowly. Trying to think of something to say.

"Hey, wait a minute," I call, like an idiot. She stops at the landing. "What . . . ah . . . where are you going?"

"Lunch." She doesn't look back at me. "That's where I usually go at lunch time."

"Sure." I smile like a jerk. "Do you mind if I . . . walk with you?"

"It's a free world." She starts up the steps.

"I mean . . . I meant, will you have lunch with me?"

She stops on the middle landing. Rests her hand on the banister and looks at me. For the first time in weeks. Her eyes those tiny blue flames.

"Why?" she asks.

Why? I should know why. But I'm not sure I do. "I just thought, you know, we haven't talked much . . . for a long time, and it's just . . ."

"Just what?"

"Just that I thought you might want to talk or something." I shrug my shoulders.

"About what?"

"About . . . ah . . . nothing."

"You want to talk about nothing?"

No. I don't want to talk about nothing. I want to tell her what happened. That's what I want to talk about. "Jenny . . . ," I mumble. "There's something I've gotta tell you."

The sky is dark blue. The branches of trees are red and swollen. The snow on the ground is melting. We stand next to the ice-filled river. Mist all around us. Our breath curling out of our mouths and drifting out over the river. I stand there telling her about Resnick. About all the things I tried to forget. About Vinny and Patrick. About me. And she just stands there. In her long gray coat. Her black hair blowing back from her face. Just stands there and stares at me. Her eyes watering in the mist.

"Why didn't you tell me?" she finally asks.

"Don't you understand? Because I can't stand to even think about it. And tomorrow I've got to do some dumb testimony."

"But, Mac." She touches my hand with her glove. "You could have talked to me."

"Jenny, I can barely talk to you now. I was scared. And I was mostly scared when I was with you."

"Scared of me?"

"Yeah, scared of you. Scared that you knew. That I disgusted . . . that you hated me."

"I never hated you. At least, not until you started hating me."

"I was scared of you. I didn't hate you. Don't you understand the difference?" I look up from the snow and try to find her blue eyes. But she's staring out over the river. "I'm sorry."

"I'm sorry, too." She looks up at me. Her blue eyes still

watering. Small drops spilling off her cheeks, like tears. "So what do we do now?" She bites her lower lip.

"I don't know." I look down at her boots. Like they should tell me what to say. Then I look back at her and the mist swirling in around us. "So —"

"So," she interrupts. "I'm freezing to death." She pulls away from me and starts back up the path. Her boots sloshing through the snow. And I just stand there. Frozen in place. Watching her go. A flock of little birds dart between us. And for no reason at all I think of Peter being a dog. And just like that it's clear to me. If he can be a dog, why the hell can't I at least be a kid? I start after her. Slowly at first. Then running as fast as my legs will go through the melting snow. I don't catch her until the soccer field. She doesn't say anything. Just reaches down to her side. And touches my bare hand with her glove. I take a few steps. A deep breath. And then ask, "Would you like to go to the movies this Friday?"

"With who?"

"With me, Jenny."

She stops walking. Takes my other hand. And looks right at me. So all I see is the blue of her eyes. "I thought you'd never ask."

• 56 •

I stare out the window. It's gray and overcast. The kind of morning trees look like shadows. Mrs. Resnick is standing at her desk talking in whispers with the social worker from the D.A.'s office. She looks like Resnick's sister. I look at the tape recorder on the table. And pick up an old *National Geographic.* I thumb through glossy pictures of coral fish. Camels of the Sahara. By the time I get to the wild dogs of India I hear Resnick clear her throat. When I look up they're both sitting around me.

"Sorry we've taken so long, Mac." Resnick has her hair pulled back tight in a ponytail. "We were just reaching an understanding. This is Mrs. Litano from the district attorney's office. She has some questions she needs to ask you." I put down the magazine. And look at her. She smiles. Pushes her big glasses up on her nose. Then talks to me with a voice so soft I can barely hear her.

"This shouldn't take long, Mac. Just a couple of questions I need to ask. None of these questions are intended to embarrass you, but some of them might. If they do, and you would rather answer them in writing, that would be fine."

"And show you what a lousy speller I am."

"Okay." She half smiles. Not sure if I'm serious or joking or both. "Are you ready then?" She reaches over and turns on the tape recorder. "The first question I have to ask you is why you were seeing this doctor."

"For a physical."

"Isn't November a little late in the year to be getting your school physical?"

"I hate physicals. They're stupid and a waste of time."

"I see. So why did you go?"

"I was told to."

"By whom?"

"The school."

"So you went to this physical reluctantly?"

I nod my head.

"Say it, Mac," Litano instructs. "The recorder can't pick up head-nodding."

"It wasn't my choice. Okay?" I can feel Mrs. Resnick looking at me.

"All right. Now I'm going to help you think back to that day, Mac. You were in the examination room. The doctor came in. Was there anyone else in the room?"

"No."

"You're sure of that?"

"Yes."

"Okay. Now, when the doctor came in, were you undressed?"

"No."

"Did the nurse ask you to undress when she took you into the examination room?"

"Yes."

"But you didn't. How come?"

"I don't know." I pick up the *National Geographic* and thumb through it.

"Mac, can you answer that question?"

"I guess." I look quickly at Mrs. Resnick, then at the rug. "I guess I was embarrassed."

"About taking off your clothes?"

"Yes."

"Why?"

"Why?" I throw the magazine across the room. "What

a dumb question! I don't like to be naked in front of other people. Is that so weird? I mean, you don't have to be a genius to understand that. Do you?"

"No, Mac. I don't have to be a genius." She clears her throat. "Just a few more questions."

"Oh, great."

"They may be the hardest for you, Mac," Mrs. Resnick warns me.

"Just great."

"So when the doctor came into the room he asked you to undress?"

"Yeah." I can feel sweat beading around my mouth. Dripping down my spine like tears. I look down at my feet. Afraid to look up.

"You undressed to your underwear?"

"Yes."

"Then he told you to take off your underwear?"

"Yes."

"And what did the doctor actually say to you when he told you to take off your underwear?"

"What do you mean, what did he say? He said something . . . something stupid like, I need to see all of you."

"And then?" she asks.

"And then," I shout at her, "you know what happened next."

"I know."

"So why are you asking me?" I shout so loud my throat feels inside out.

"Mac." Mrs. Resnick puts her arm around my shoulders. She's so close I can see the freckles on her eyelids. I push away from her.

"Just one more question, Mac."

"No more questions, Edith. Don't you have enough?"

"I'm afraid not." Her voice is so soft it disappears.

"Well, you'll have to wait a minute."

"I'll wait." Someone hands me a Kleenex. I blow my nose and sit up. "I know it's painful, Mac, recalling all of this. Especially in front of us. All I can say to help you is that this can put an end to this doctor's awful practice. And that, in the long run, this type of confession will be helpful to you."

"I have nothing to confess," I shout at her.

"That's not what she meant, Mac." Mrs. Resnick nudges me with her elbow. "She meant disclosure. And she meant that talking about an awful experience can help you understand it." I don't answer her. But ball up the Kleenex. And throw it in the wastebasket. And then for a long time no one says anything.

"Mac, all I need is one more question answered. Are you ready?" I don't look at her. "Before the doctor touched you, did he say anything?"

I nod my head.

"Do you remember what he said, Mac?"

"Yes, I remember."

"Go on, Mac. It's almost over. I promise you."

"He said . . . he said, I want to test . . . all of your reactions. It's a part of . . . examining teenage boys."

"And then he touched your genitals?"

"Yes," I shout, covering my face with my hands.

"And then he touched you with his genitals?"

"So what if he did?"

"Yes or no, Mac."

"That's enough, Edith."

"Yes. The dirty bastard did."

"That's it." She clicks off the tape recorder.

• 57 •

I watch her take the tape recorder from Resnick and the door close behind her. Like it never happened.

"Well, that was something." She walks back across the room towards me. "A few questions, indeed." She sits down next to me. "How do you feel?"

I don't answer. Just sit there. Like after a game we just lost. "What's going to happen to the bastard?" I finally ask.

"I don't know, Mac."

"Will they throw his ass in jail?"

"Could be. Would that make you happy?"

"Yeah." It would make me happy, I think. Sort of. I stare out the window for a while. At the clouds breaking up.

"How do you feel, Mac?"

"Tired." So tired I don't even look at her.

"I don't blame you. She sure put you through the wringer. And you," she says, putting her arm around my shoulders, "are amazingly courageous."

58

After the movie Jenny and I walk up past Baker's drugstore, the front windows all steamed up. Past the super-
market, the town hall, the library. All dark and closed up
for the night. It doesn't take long to walk through this
town. I follow her around to the back door of her house.
The kitchen light is on. We take off our coats and drop
them on the closet floor.

"Want to hear something?" she asks, walking into the
other room.

"Sure." I get a glass of water and follow her into the
living room. She's already put on a tape. Before the song
starts I hear the speakers at the end of the couch, hissing
under spider plants. It's Dire Straits. The bass guitar rolls
out of the speakers. Cymbals like rain. And that voice
sadder than life.

> *Here I am again in this mean old town.*
> *And you're so far away . . .*
> *So far I just can't see . . .*
> *So far away from me.*

I turn and look at Jenny. The music's so loud it makes
the room seem huge. The couch a runway. Jenny at the
far end, a thousand miles away. She turns and looks at me.
I turn away. Like I'm going to take off. I get up. And lie
down on the Oriental rug. Close my eyes and listen. The
floor vibrating. In between songs the house is silent. Except for the furnace rumbling. The radiators clanking.

And Jenny's stocking feet walking across the floor to the
tape deck. She turns it off. Then sits next to me. On the
floor. Looking right at me. Those blue eyes. Under her
black hair. Like stars.

"Why'd you turn it off?"

"Because I want to talk."

"About what?"

"About you being such a nerd."

"I'm not a nerd."

"You're acting like one. All night long. Like you're pretending I'm not around. I don't like it, Mac."

"I'm sorry."

"I thought you were your old self again."

"I never said that." I look right at her. "I never said I
was my old self. I just told you what I've been through. I
don't know if I'll ever be my old self again."

"Terrific. You mean you're going to be a creep forever."

"I'm not a creep."

"Yes, you are. All you can think about is yourself."

"Bullshit."

"Like the only thing in the world that matters is Mac's
feelings. Well, I have news for you, Mac. There are other
things in this world besides your feelings. And there are
other people, too."

"You don't have to yell, Jenny. I know there're other
people."

"No, you don't. But you used to. That's what I liked
about you. You used to really care about other people. It
was right there in your eyes."

"My eyes?" I look down at the rug.

"But it's not there now. Now all I see is Big Mac this, Big Mac that. Like you're a cheeseburger or something." She laughs.

"That's not funny, Jenny."

"Big Mac." She laughs again. "I swore I'd never say that in front of you. But you've been such a Big Ass Mac." She leans towards me, laughing so hard her head bounces up and down.

"You're a riot, Jenny." I try not to laugh but I can't help it. Just looking at her laughing makes me laugh. And laugh. Until I think I'm going to cry.

When we finally stop laughing, she gets up off the floor and goes to the tape deck. Flips it on. And sits down next to me. Dire Straits breaks into their last song. Gentle guitar. Thrilling up and down the spine. And a synthesizer. Sweeter than flutes.

> *I see this world has made you sad*
> *Some people can be bad*
> *The things they do, the things they say*
> *But, baby . . .*
> *There should be laughter after pain.*
> *There should be sunshine after rain.*

Her hand circles my fist. I look at her. She smiles that smile of hers. I smile back. Close-lipped. Awkward and embarrassed. The smell of her soft skin like a dream I'll never forget.

59

The next thing I know the room is lit up by headlights. And a car is roaring up the driveway.

"Wake up, Mac. Wake up. It's my mother."

"What time is it?"

"It doesn't matter. You're not supposed to be here." She's grabbing me by the hand. "You've got to hide."

"Where?"

She pulls me into the front hall. "Upstairs. No." She stops.

"In the cellar. That's it." The car door slams and footsteps start towards the back of the house.

"You're sure that's your mother?"

"Stop being stupid. Of course it's my mother. Now, come on." She pulls me towards the kitchen. But by the time we get to the living room there are steps on the back porch.

"Oh, shit. Too late for the cellar. Upstairs." She spins me around and pulls me up the stairs. "Quick. Quick."

"I'm coming. I'm coming."

"Hush." She pulls me down the hall and into a room. "Under the bed."

"What?"

"Get under the bed!"

She pulls up the white dust-ruffle and shoves me. "Quick. Quick, I tell you." I get down on my knees. And squeeze under the bed. Pulling with my elbows. She tiptoes into the hall. I hear a click. And a faint light filters under the bed. I pivot around on my belly so I can see the doorway. She tiptoes back in the room. Her feet only inches from my face.

"What are you doing?" I whisper.

"Hush." Her feet disappear under a pile of blue jeans, then step out of the pile. Naked. I lean forward but the feet disappear. And the bed springs squish down around my head.

"What are you doing?" I whisper.

"What do you mean, what am I doing?" she whispers back. "I'm getting in bed. Now, be quiet. If my mother finds you here we're dead."

Terrific. I put my hands together. Oh, God, please, please don't let her find me. Please, please don't let her come in here. When I dare to look up I see a pair of gray shoes in the doorway. Pointing sideways. I don't dare breathe. I watch the shoes slowly turn and start across the rug towards the bed.

"You asleep, honey?" Her voice is like Jenny's. Her shoes are only inches from my face.

"Huh?" Jenny mumbles like she's asleep.

"I got you something at the auction." I lean away from the shoes. Like they have eyes that can see me. She sits down on the bed. And the sagging springs press my face against the floor.

"Guess what I got you?"

"I can't."

"I know you can't. It's too wonderful for words. For only a hundred dollars I bought you the right to work in a lawyer's office over spring break."

"You what?" Jenny sounds wide awake now.

"Isn't that great, hon?"

"That's not great, Mom. That's dumb. I mean, you don't pay people to work for them. They pay you."

"Not with the spring auction, hon. It's all for a good cause."

"Mom!"

"We'll talk about it in the morning, hon. I'm too exhausted now. Good night, dear." She gets off the bed and the springs lift up off my head.

I watch the back of her shoes walk out of the room. Then I hear them click down the hallway and a door closing. Then nothing.

"Do you believe that?" Jenny whispers angrily. "She pays to have me work. I tell you, that woman drives me crazy."

I don't say anything. I just sigh. And let my face drop to the floor. Close my eyes and wonder how the hell I'm ever going to get out of here.

"Jenny?" I whisper. "What time is it?"

"Shhh." The springs squeak. "One-thirty."

"I've got to get home." I start to squirm out from under the bed.

"Shhh. Wait." Her hand swoops down and grabs the pile of blue jeans. "Stay there," she whispers. I don't move. The springs squeak. Then both her feet are on the floor and she's kneeling next to the bed. Looking at me in the faint light.

"Be quiet," she whispers. Then she gets up. Goes to the door and shuts it so the room is totally dark. I stretch out my arms. Lift my shoulders off the floor. And slowly pull my legs out from under the bed. I'm just about to stand up when Jenny knocks into me. I fall down and she lands on top of me.

"What are you doing?"

"Shhh. I didn't see you." I can feel her breath against my cheek.

"I've gotta get out of here."

"Mac, if you don't whisper we're both going to get killed." Her nose brushes against my cheek.

"What'll we do?" I whisper.

"In a minute we'll sneak downstairs . . . when Mom's asleep."

I turn my head to say something and my mouth brushes her lips.

"What are you doing?" she whispers.

"Nothing," I whisper back.

"Yes, you are. You're kissing me."

"No, I'm not." I push my mouth against hers.

She doesn't say anything. But presses her mouth harder against mine. I put my arms around her and pull her tightly to me.

• 60 •

I don't know how long we lie there kissing. Long after my mouth starts aching. And long after the first light filters through the curtains. Even after sunlight spills through the windows we keep kissing. It's like if we were to stop kissing we would stop breathing.

Jenny's the first to talk. She whispers around my lips. "You have to get out of here."

I nod my head. But how can I leave? With this girl in my arms? Her tongue curled around mine? Her legs wrapped around my legs?

"You've got to get out of here," she whispers again. "This is ridiculous. It's morning."

"I know."

Slowly we pull apart. She gets on her knees and pulls me up. Then wraps her arms around me and we kiss some more.

"Come on." She pushes me towards the door. Stops and grabs her Walkman off the bureau. Hangs it over her shoulder. And pulls open the door. There isn't a sound. We tiptoe out onto the landing. Down the stairs. Through the living room. In the bathroom off the kitchen, I watch her brush her hair.

"Look at me." I look at her. "You're a mess." She pulls the brush through my hair. "That's better. Now brush your teeth."

"With what?"

"Your finger." She turns on the water so it trickles out of the faucet. And scrubs her teeth with her finger. I do the same. Then we pick our parkas up off the closet floor. And step out into the morning light.

We run on tiptoes out the driveway. And down the road to the corner where we stop, out of breath. "I can't believe you did that, Mac."

"Did what?"

"I can't believe you spent the entire night in my room."

She laughs into her hand. "If my mother finds out she'll kill us."

"Mine too. I guess . . ." I look down at the cracks on the sidewalk. "I guess this kind of means . . . we're sort of going together again?"

"I guess so." She looks at me. The whole sky reflected in her eyes. And I just stand there. Like a jerk. Staring at her.

"What do you want to do?"

"Want to just walk?"

"Sure." And we start down the sidewalk. I open my hand and her fingers slip between mine. The sun breaks through the clouds behind us. And all around us are trees. On fire in the first morning sun.